The Other Side of the Flood

The *The* Other Side *of the* Flood

———— ⚜ ————

JOSHUA 24:14-15

Sarah Kelly Albritton

WESTBOW
PRESS
A DIVISION OF THOMAS NELSON

WestBow Press books may be ordered through booksellers or by contacting:

WestBow Press
A Division of Thomas Nelson
1663 Liberty Drive
Bloomington, IN 47403
www.westbowpress.com
1-(866) 928-1240

Scripture taken from the King James Version. Copyright 1997 by Cornerstone Bible Publishers, Nashville, Tennessee. Used by permission. All rights reserved.

ISBN: 978-1-4497-8071-5 (sc)
ISBN: 978-1-4497-8072-2 (hc)
ISBN: 978-1-4497-8070-8 (e)

Library of Congress Control Number: 2012924217

Printed in the United States of America

WestBow Press rev. date: 1/7/2013

Introduction

It was the spring of 1809 when John Torrey and his young wife, Effie, left North Carolina with all their worldly goods. They had sold all of their land and timber on the Lumber River in Robeson County, trusting that this money would be sufficient to build a comfortable home and purchase servants to help cultivate the new land.

They made their way through Tennessee into Mississippi Territory in wagons with four other families who were related to them through marriage and their strong faith. Alongside the Torrey family, the Buies, McEacherns, Gilchrists, and Graftons made their way through rough terrain and inclement weather to the flat land of Mississippi.

Their primary goal was to settle in an area where they could worship their God and properly educate their children. They moved into a little community called Scotland, where the main buildings were a small Presbyterian church and a one-room schoolhouse. Each family was dedicated to its Scottish roots and the religious education of the children. The people of the community were of the same mind and welcomed the new families with open arms.

John Torrey purchased land for his family and immediately began to prepare for the construction of his new home. In 1820, George Edward Torrey was born to John and Effie. The boy was only seven when his father fell ill with a fever and died, but his mother was a strong woman. She had overcome many adversities since arriving in

Mississippi. She had lost her twins, John and James, when they were very young, and then her husband. Her life is a testimony to the strong faith and determination of these resilient people.

Chapter 1

It was a typical day in the August of 1858. Thunder rumbled across the flat land as dark clouds assembled in the distance. "I smell rain," Elizabeth Torrey whispered to herself as she sat, legs crossed, in a huge white wicker chair on the front porch. She sat quietly, watching the dark clouds roll slowly toward her plantation home as the cooling breeze crossed her face. It had been extremely hot and humid all week; a nice, cool rain would be welcomed.

A young girl of four appeared and stepped carefully through the tall window that opened all the way to the floor. These windows were raised to allow for any cool breeze that might stir in summer. "Mama says come inside 'cause bad weather is coming this way." Dark curls bounced as Anna Jane Torrey hopped first on one foot and then the other. Her face was a round, angelic frame for her enormous dark brown eyes.

"Mama worries too much." These pearls of wisdom came from the nymph-like figure of the seven-year-old in the wicker chair. With her long limbs still folded and white pantaloons exposed, she continued gazing pensively into the lowering skies.

"Papa says that at the first sign of trouble, we all need to run to the pea patch 'cause peas have saved our lives so many times before. What's that mean, Elizabeth? How can peas save a person's life?" Anna's big brown eyes widened even more as she waited expectantly for Elizabeth to answer.

"Be still, Anna, and listen to the thunder. The Devil is beating his wife."

"That's not true, Elizabeth," she whined.

"It's just like the Noah flood that Papa read to us out of the Bible," Elizabeth continued. "Does that scare you, Anna?" Her voice was almost a whisper.

"No, Miss Smarty, that was for bad people who didn't obey God. Let's go inside. I smell hoecakes."

Easing herself out of the chair, Elizabeth stepped through the window. She waited to help her little sister crawl back through before closing the window to keep out any rain that might blow in through the opening.

It was cool on the polished oak floor inside the parlor. The house seemed smaller as the clouds began to roll in and cover all traces of the sun like a blanket being pulled across the parlor floor. The whole parlor smelled of the honeysuckle and jasmine Mama had picked and arranged in the crystal vase on the dining room table. The vase had belonged to Grandma Effie, who had died before the girls were born.

Their bare feet made no sound as the two crossed the shiny parlor floor to the long hallway leading into the kitchen. Grandpa Torrey had the kitchen built on the north end of the house to aid in heating it when the cold winter months came. Grandpa had amassed considerable wealth from the sale of his land and timber in North Carolina. The money had afforded him the means to build his family a relatively large home with enough laborers to work the fields and do the cooking and cleaning in the main house.

Izzy was the inside servant who took care of the cooking and the cleaning. She had been present to help deliver George when he was born. No one really knew what Izzy's original name was, but they presumed it must have been Elizabeth. When Izzy felt she could use extra help, she enlisted the help of a wife of one of the field hands. She did not like others in her kitchen, and for this reason, she very seldom asked for help with anything except the cleaning. Izzy's daughter, Simmy, helped her with some of the duties in the main house. Izzy and Simmy shared a large room just off the kitchen in the main house.

Izzy had come to the home with her husband, Isaac, after they were purchased at the slave auction in New Orleans. Also among the several slaves Grandpa Torrey purchased was one young woman who became pregnant years later and died in childbirth. Having no children of their own, Izzy and Isaac took the baby and raised her. No one knew where Izzy got the name Simmy, and she never offered to explain. They had only had Simmy for a month when Isaac was killed while helping to clear the land for planting. A falling tree crushed him, leaving Izzy and Simmy alone. They both lived in the main house since that time.

Izzy mopped her dark brown face with a white cloth as the girls approached. She was laboring over the wood-burning stove, preparing the evening meal for the family. She was not tall, barely five feet, but she had a presence about her. She had endured many hard times but remained proud and strong. She wore a dark cotton dress and a white apron that was tied in the back slightly higher than where her waist would have been. The girls loved to hug her but could never reach more than halfway around her portly frame.

She was preparing fried chicken, peas with okra, corn on the cob, and hoecakes for the evening meal. The hoecakes were made with fresh ground meal, eggs from their own chickens, milk from Bitterweed, their cow, and just a smidgen of sugar. The batter was dropped from a spoon into a large black skillet on the stove. Lard heated to smoking was used for frying the cakes quickly to a crunchy, golden brown.

As Anna walked by Izzy's work table, where the first hoecakes had been removed from the skillet and placed to cool, she slowed her pace. Reaching to the table, she pinched off the crusty end of one of the cakes and grabbed another with her empty hand. Elizabeth followed suit. "You chillin', get outta my kitchen for I gets me a switch!" Izzy's bark was much worse than her bite, and although she was quite loud, she never scared the girls. Hearing the giggles as the girls ran down the long hall, Izzy smiled. "Oh Lord, them gals gonna be the death o' me."

Papa was reading his Bible in the west room beside the great window that Grandpa had shipped from Europe. It was clear, very heavy glass with deep red edges and outlined in scrolls of gold filigree. According to Papa, it was very expensive, and great care should be taken when little people played in the west room.

Anna poked her little face around the door frame and looked into the west room at her father until she saw him close his Bible. He was a tall, strong man with a well-trimmed mustache. His eyes were dark and kind and shone as if they were smiling all the time. Even in August, he wore a long-sleeved shirt with the sleeves rolled up to the elbow. In the winter, he would simply roll the sleeves down for warmth. Being a Scotsman, he was true to the tradition of being frugal. He was a very pious man and well-respected in the community. He was dedicated to looking after the religious training of his children and bringing them up in the nurture and admonition of the Lord. Being a staunch Presbyterian, he made sure they learned their catechism and understood their Calvinistic doctrine of being chosen by the Father, called by the Holy Spirit, and saved by the blood of Jesus.

"Papa?" Anna Jane made her voice sound as sweet as she possibly could. "Elizabeth says that God is sending a Noah flood." She was not truly afraid but wanted the attention of the man she admired most in the world. This is a tactic learned very early by Southern women.

"Anna, come here," her father answered. Hoecake in hand, she bounded across the room with her arms held out toward her father in anticipation of being scooped up and placed on his knees.

Spying the hoecake in her hand and the little grease spots on her pinafore, he peered at her over his wire-rimmed glasses. Realizing that she had forgotten all about the hoecake in her hand, her little arms went to her side. "Anna, what is this in your hand?"

"Hoecake, Papa." Her eyes dropped to the dark oak floor. Little tears began to well up in her brown eyes—not from fear of her father but the possibility of disappointing him.

"Did you take it from the kitchen, or did Izzy give it to you?"

"I took it, Papa." Anna had learned early on that lying was not tolerated in the Torrey home and was always punished. Satisfied with the truth, Papa leaned forward, embraced Anna—grease and all—and placed her on his knees. The feeling that came over Anna was that of purest love and awe. *My papa,* she thought. *I love you so much.*

The next morning, the sun rose bright and warm. Elizabeth and Anna were awakened by the smell of bacon and eggs frying in the big black skillet and Izzy's delicious buttermilk biscuits baking in the oven. The smell of coffee heating on the stove, combined with all the other wonderful aromas, announced to everyone that breakfast time was at hand. The girls crawled lazily out of bed to find two little wash basins that mama had filled with water. The cool water on their faces revived them as they washed the sleep from their eyes and bounced downstairs, still in their little cotton nightgowns.

Mama had already dressed in her blue gingham dress. She was a beautiful young woman, eight years her husband's junior. Her hair was pulled up on top of her head in a bun but not too severe. This accented her long, graceful neck. Her eyes were intensely blue but very kind and knowing.

Papa appeared and seated himself at the head of the table. In front of him was a steaming cup of coffee that had been placed there by mama. This was everyone's cue to be seated. Head bowed, Papa began. "Gracious Lord, pardon our sins, and accept our thanks for these and all Thy many blessings. In Jesus' name. Amen."

As the *amen* sounded, Izzy appeared with a large platter of bacon and eggs and a bowl of grits with butter. Simmy, Izzy's adopted daughter, followed her mother with hot buttered biscuits and a little dish of fig preserves, placing them on the table. Mama and Papa served their own plates while Izzy fixed a plate for each little girl to insure that they received just the right amount of everything.

Papa talked of making repairs to some of the cottages in the slave quarters behind the main house. He wanted to be sure they were well insulated against the cold when winter came. There were twelve little cottages out back in which to house the servants and field hands. Grandpa Torrey's idea was that the twelve cottages he built would represent the twelve tribes of Israel, and he named them accordingly. Elizabeth and Anna could not pronounce all the tribe names and suggested changing them from the names of the twelve tribes to the names of the twelve apostles. This idea was not without merit, but there was one small problem. Nobody wanted to live in the cottage named Judas.

After breakfast, the girls went upstairs and changed into little cotton dresses for playing outside. Once down the high, wooden steps leading to the backyard from the kitchen, the girls headed for the garden. There were long rows of corn, pole beans, okra, tomatoes, cucumbers climbing on the fence, and a short row of green onions. To the side of the garden was the infamous, life-saving pea patch that on occasion had provided excellent cover for a snake or two. Being careful to avoid the pea patch, they headed for the long rows of corn in search of the smaller ears with long strands of corn silk emanating from the top. Once pulled, the young ears of corn were transformed into little dolls with long, silken hair. The corn babies were put to bed on the soft, green moss that grew beneath the big oak tree and given carriage rides in an old cigar box that had once belonged to Grandpa Torrey.

"I'm tired of these babies," Anna said after some time and much nurturing of the now-dirty corn. "Besides, all my baby's hair fell out. I think she must have a terrible disease or even fleas." Throwing the dolls to the side, the two girls scampered through the yard like playful puppies, searching out the great places to play on the grounds of Tehvah. The giant old oak with the grey Spanish moss hanging from the branches and bright green moss growing around the roots on the ground piqued the imagination. It was a magical place.

"Izzy said that once a horse thief was hung in this very tree," Elizabeth said in hushed tones, as was her custom when she was about to spin some yarn designed to scare her little sister. They sat down reverently on the soft moss beneath the tree and quietly surveyed the scene. If the truth were known, Elizabeth had made herself a little uneasy with the hanging story.

Behind them were the twelve little cottages, all neat with whitewash, and to the right was a wrought iron fence surrounding a plot of land with four white tombstones resting inside. The Scottish traditionally buried their people on their own land, and this was the Torrey family plot. The four graves belonged to Grandpa John, Grandma Effie, and their two other sons, born before their own papa. The boys, John and James, were twins and had died in their first year of life after contracting diphtheria. They died within a week of each other. Elizabeth and Anna made their way over to the family plot and looked sadly at the two small tombstones, which were especially bothersome to them. The stones were small and had pictures of lambs carved into them. Each stone had the child's name with the date of his birth and death. The Scripture was the same on each child's marker and read, "Suffer the little children to come unto me and forbid them not for of such is the kingdom of heaven. Mark 10:14"

The girls were silent but only for a short while. At four years old, Anna's attention span was not very long unless Papa was doing the talking. "Why don't we talk to Grandpa and Grandma, Elizabeth?" It made Anna feel quite stoic to speak of talking to the dead.

"You didn't even know Grandma and Grandpa, Anna—and besides, they can't hear you, silly."

"Well, you don't know, Elizabeth," she said, losing her melancholy mood. "Mr. Lazarus heard Jesus call him, and he got right up from being dead and walked on out of his tomb."

"Well, Anna Jane, that's all well and good, but you ain't *Jesus*."

Chapter 2

The year 1858 was good for the Torrey household. The cotton was harvested and on the way to market by mid-September. The field hands had to hoe the weeds only once, which made for happier workers. There was much singing in the fields as the workers picked the cotton. The words of old spirituals rose from the fields like the winds of March lifting whirling clouds of dust from the dry, newly plowed field. Songs filled the air in melodious harmony. They sang about Moses in Egypt land with the enslaved Israelites, and they sang about crossing over the Jordan into campground. They sang happily, unaware of the terrible price that would be paid in only a few short years for their own freedom.

The family garden was bountiful, and Mama and Izzy had put up tomatoes, pole beans, pepper sauce, and pickles and made delicious fig preserves. Muscadines had been harvested from the nearby woods to make jelly. These canned foods would help see them all through the winter.

The little creek that ran beside the cotton field had been a blessing both for irrigation of the crops and for relief on hot summer days when the girls refreshed themselves by splashing and wading in it. The creek had become a favorite place to play for Elizabeth, Anna, and Simmy. Simmy was ten years older than Elizabeth, and one of her assigned duties was to keep a close watch on Anna and Elizabeth.

The creek could be dangerous—not because it was deep, but because of the poisonous snakes that sometimes enjoyed a cool dip. Last year, the snakes were not numerous, because there was plenty of rain, but too little rain would bring them out.

On this day in April, 1859, Elizabeth, Anna, and Simmy were playing near the creek in back of the house, where they could see the cotton fields that had been plowed and planted with the next crop. At Tehvah, life was good. The almanac had said that the time for frost was past, and Papa had the garden planted earlier than usual. The tender green tomato plants were already peeking up from the rich, black Mississippi soil. George Torrey trusted in the Lord to supply their needs but felt it wise to use the information that the Lord had provided.

It was still too cool for the girls to wade in the creek, even though they had ventured outside without Izzy's knowledge and without their shoes. On their way to the creek, they had filled their apron pockets with rocks from the path, because they had plans to disrupt the long, lazy day lives of the turtles that crawled upon logs to sun themselves.

They passed the family cemetery, holding their breath (for reasons known only to them) and walked between the houses of Benjamin and Joseph toward the creek. Simmy led the way, watching out for any signs of danger that may be in their way. She was ready to sacrifice her own safety for her little friends—or so she thought. Simmy was a very tall girl of seventeen and much darker than Izzy, with large, full lips; a slightly broad nose; and narrow, very dark eyes. She could spin a yarn almost as well as Izzy, and for that reason, Elizabeth and Anna could never quite distinguish between the truth and the fiction of her tales.

She told them that her grandpa was a big African chief. "Folks'd bow down on they knees and bring 'im gifts jut like them wise mens brung Jesus. They'd bring spice and gold pieces and real true heads cut offen' folks they'd war with." Elizabeth didn't believe a word and thought it the biggest tale of Simmy's storytelling career. Anna wondered about it and imagined a great African man, painted like a wild Indian, surrounded by severed heads. *Who would want something like that?* she wondered.

Elizabeth reached into her apron pocket and selected a nice-sized round stone. As she hurled it at one of the larger turtles on the log, she chanted, "Ol' Mr. Turtle, go home to your wife. If you tarry here long, you'll surely lose your life." The turtle slid into the water, causing tiny ripples to spread over the surface of the creek. Anna didn't much like the idea of turtle-killing, so she just skipped her rocks harmlessly across the water.

"That's all you gonna do with your rocks, Anna?" Simmy thought it a waste of good rocks and energy. Tired of the turtle killing-efforts and the rock-skipping, the three sat down on the soft, clean moss by the creek.

Anna moved closer to Simmy and rubbed her hand across Simmy's dark skin on her arm. "Simmy, why did God make you this color?"

"Anna," her sister scolded, but   secretly she wanted to know what Simmy thought.

"Aw, I don't know; wondered thet myself lots of times, but it don't make me no worsen' nobody else, just different from you."

Encouraged by Simmy's soft answer, Elizabeth pressed on, "I heard somebody say that color was the mark of Cain." She waited for Simmy's reaction. Simmy stiffened. This was too much for Simmy. She knew the story of Cain and Abel and how Cain had killed his brother.

"Ain't no truth in that, Miss Lizbeth. That'd mean we's no better'n a bunch of killers. Just look at you trying to kill a bunch of poor ol' tutles what lives in your creek and ain't hurting nobody." Anna moved closer to the creek bank until she could feel the soft mud ooze between her toes. Quietly, she stooped down and stirred the thick, black mud on the bank with her fingers. Elizabeth and Simmy fell silent, paying no attention to Anna and pouting about each calling the other a murderer.

Anna crawled up quietly from the creek bank until she faced the other two. Jumping quickly to her feet, she stood tall in front of them, her face covered completely with the thick, black Mississippi mud. Only the whites of her big, bright eyes showed. Elizabeth and Simmy stared at Anna, stunned in their disbelief. Then came the finale when Anna smiled her biggest smile, adding bright white teeth to her transformed face. Not daring to speak, Elizabeth looked at Simmy. Her face showed no emotion except that of pure surprise, and then Simmy fell backward on the ground. Peals of laughter came from deep within her soul. Relieved, Elizabeth fell back with Simmy and laughed.

"I swear, Anna, if you ain't the ugliest li'l darkie I ever laid my eyes on." All three rolled on the soft moss and laughed till the tears came. After washing Anna's new face off, the three started home, but this time arm-in-arm.

That afternoon after catechism lesson was over, Papa asked that the family fetch Izzy and Simmy and come into the parlor. When they had all assembled, Papa asked that they all bow their heads for prayer. A special family meeting usually meant something bad had happened or there was a special need for which to pray. Papa began, "Oh Lord, infinite, eternal, and unchangeable …" (Elizabeth recognized these words from the shorter catechism.) "Your mercy is everlasting, and your truth endureth to all generations."

Simmy silently prayed that her color was not related to the mark of Cain and that the turtles Elizabeth hit, if any, would not die. Then the vision of Anna's face at the creek appeared to her and she smiled. She ventured a peek to make sure that no one saw her.

Papa continued, "We thank you for all our blessings of the past year of good health, good crops, and for spiritual guidance. This year, we also thank you for our family and for the addition to it. We pray that you will bless Mama with good health and a strong, healthy baby. In Jesus' name. Amen."

"What?" Elizabeth almost shouted. "Papa, do you mean that Mama is having a little baby?"

Papa smiled. "Yes, Elizabeth. Are you excited?"

"Oh, yes, Papa."

Then Papa turned his attention to his youngest daughter. "Well, Anna, you are very quiet. Are you happy?"

"I guess so, Papa," she replied, but her heart ached at the thought of having to share Papa with another child and no longer being Papa's baby. She was having great difficulty handling her emotions, and she stepped quietly out of the parlor, down the hall, and upstairs to her bedroom.

Anna laid across her canopy bed, buried her face in the pillow, and sobbed. She did not hear the soft footsteps as they came silently into the room. Someone sat down easily on her bed, smoothing her long, curly hair. She knew that touch. Turning, she sobbed, "Papa."

He pulled her close and placed his chin on her curls, as he had done when she came in with the greasy hoe cake. He whispered to her softly, "Anna, who made you?"

Remembering her first catechism question, Anna softly replied, "God did, Papa."

He gave her another squeeze and continued, "And God has made you a little brother or sister to love. Do we reject what God gives us, Anna?"

"No, Papa." She sniffed and looked into his kind eyes. Once again, her father had shown her how much he loved her, and all seemed right with the world.

The two went back down to the parlor to join the rest of the family members, where Mama smiled down at Anna and enlisted her help with the new baby when it arrived. Simmy silently took Anna's hand and smiled sweetly into the little face. Anna felt her love.

It was almost supper time when the evening catechism class ended. Anna tried desperately to learn the answer to the question, "What is sin?" She wanted to get a jump on the shorter catechism to keep up with Elizabeth. She had trouble with "the want of conformity" but better understood "the transgression of the law of God." Elizabeth had moved onto the first question in the shorter catechism.

Simmy was still thinking about the verse in the Bible that George Torrey had read to them that morning: "Greater love hath no man than this, that he lay down his life for his friends." Simmy sat in on the Catechism classes but was not such a willing participant. After all, she was a Baptist. Izzy thought any kind of Bible study would be beneficial, but the stories from the Bible were a lot more interesting to Simmy. But it was supper time, and Simmy was hungry.

Simmy could smell the chicken and dumplings cooking on the stove and visualized the big black pot with tender white dumplings and generous pieces of chicken swimming in large portions of butter and cream. The thing that always bothered Simmy was seeing the skinny yellow chicken feet sticking up amid all that savory goodness. She could never understand why Izzy cooked the feet, because they surely had no meat on them. One day, she asked her mother why she served the chicken feet in her stew. Izzy told her, "Them feets for flavor and for greedy folk that wants more than they share." Simmy never questioned her mother's reasoning; she simply dipped around the yellow feet and left them for the gluttons. It was funny that there seemed to be no gluttons at the Torrey table.

Izzy completed the meal by cooking some of the pole beans that they had canned, adding slices of ham from the smokehouse. She always served up her vegetables with hot corn bread, and this time, the bread was baked in a pan inside the oven. Unlike hoe cakes, this bread was called corn pone, because it was baked and cut into squares instead of being fried.

The day had been a long one, and the whole family was ready for rest. Simmy, who ate in the kitchen with Izzy, left the table, helped collect the dishes, and went wearily to her room beside the kitchen. After she put on her thin cotton gown, she knelt beside her bed, said her prayer, as she had always done, and climbed into bed. As tired as she seemed to be, she could not stop her mind from racing as she recapped the events of the day. "Lord, why'd you make some folk white and some black? Why's some folk good and some bad? Why'd my mama have to die? Who'd I give my life for? Maybe I just ask Mr. George tomorrow." Her eyes closed in peaceful sleep.

Chapter 3

It was Sunday morning, and Simmy woke to the sun peeking into her window. She knew it was the Lord's day, and she could hear Izzy already collecting her cooking utensils and pans in the kitchen. She bounded out of bed, put on her robe, and hurried into the kitchen to help Izzy with breakfast. Sunday breakfast was different from other days, because Papa was against anybody working on Sunday. The only cooking would be biscuits, ham, and gravy. Simmy would dress later for church in her very best dress, which was a gift from Flora Torrey on the occasion of Simmy's fourteenth birthday.

There was a young man among the field hands who Simmy greatly admired, and he would be at church that day. The slaves attended their own service under a spreading oak near the creek. There was a balcony in the little community church for all the slaves who wished to attend, but they preferred their own style of worship. It was a bit more enthusiastic than the structured, more formal service of the Presbyterian congregation. At Tehvah Plantation, Joshua, one of their own, had decided that the Lord had called him to preach to their congregation. Sometimes the service took on the atmosphere of Jericho when, with a mighty shout, the walls fell flat. "Nothin' wrong with getting 'cited 'bout God's power," Izzy would say.

Izzy greased two large pans and placed the hand-rolled biscuits into them. The gravy—poor man's gravy, as Grandma Effie called it—was made by browning flour in a little lard and adding water and salt. Izzy stirred the brown, bubbling mixture till it thickened and then poured it into a china bowl. One pan of biscuits was for breakfast, with sliced ham and gravy, and the other pan would be warmed up or eaten cold for lunch. There was always meat to slice from the smokehouse and preserves, jelly, and milk. This would allow everyone time to attend church.

Simmy could hardly contain her excitement as she helped clear the table after breakfast. She was thinking about Zebulon, who was named for the house in which he was born. He was a strong, dark young man who was only slightly taller than Simmy, and when she stood near him, she always stooped a little so that he would not be self-conscious about his short statue.

"I done, Mama," Simmy called over her shoulder as she hurried off to collect her wonderful dress. It was white with tiny pink roses around the yoke. She tied it at the waist with a pink satin ribbon. Her petticoat was slightly shorter than her dress but not so short as to let any sunlight through the skirt of her dress. She slipped into her white shoes and walked into the kitchen for her mother's approval. The shoes were from the year before and little bit short, but she scrunched up her toes and walked toward Izzy.

"Oh, my baby, I be lookin' at one of them angels floating round up in heaven. You a growed-up lady." Izzy's eyes filled with tears as she hugged Simmy. Simmy beamed with pride from Izzy's reaction, because more often than not, Izzy was short on compliments.

Church would be nice that day. It was Easter Sunday, and the chill had left the air. The Lord had risen, and Simmy was a lovely sight as she fairly floated nearer to the church at the big spreading oak tree and closer to Zebulon. "Hallelujah!" Simmy heard as she drew nearer. She had hoped it was Zeb's reaction upon seeing her for the first time in her wonderful finery, but alas, it was Joshua, the self-proclaimed preacher. He continued, "Jesus is risen!" It was time to begin.

There were long, wooden benches on which to sit, but Simmy did not like the thought of getting her white dress dirty on the bench, and she continued to stand. It was then that she spied Zeb walking toward her with a large white handkerchief in his hand. She felt that her heart would leap right out of its resting place. "Mornin', Miss Simmy," he said, eyeing her with great respect and admiration. Zeb unfolded the pristine white handkerchief and placed it on the wooden bench behind her.

"Thank you," Simmy said as she smiled up at him.

At the community Presbyterian church, the Torrey family arrived in their buggy. Papa drove the buggy as close to the stepping stump as possible to allow for a shorter step from buggy to ground. In this church, no one arrived late because of the placement of the pulpit inside the church. It was located directly beside the front door so that the congregation would see the late arrivals—but worse than that was the complete silence that followed until the walk to the family pew was complete.

"Christ is risen," the preacher began.

"He is risen indeed," replied the congregation. The sermon was on the nineteenth and twentieth chapters of John—the scourging of Jesus, the crucifixion, and His resurrection. Anna wondered why the Father did not reach down from heaven and rescue Jesus. She was sure He had a good reason. Elizabeth lamented her attempts to kill the turtles without knowing why she wanted them dead anyway. She silently vowed to never do that again and prayed to be forgiven. These questions and events would later be discussed with Papa.

The sermon was at last at an end. It was quite lengthy, for Reverend Grafton had to cover at least five points in his sermon. At one time, the girls had thought that the fewer points he had in his sermon, the shorter it would be. This was not the case, but each Sunday, they wondered, *Will it be a two-pointer or a six-pointer?* Somehow, they always felt more receptive to a two-point sermon.

Back at home, the family gathered for the Sunday meal. Mama did not feel well and went straight upstairs to rest. Izzy had the biscuits already warmed up and loaded the side board with sliced ham, butter, jelly, and preserves. Papa then prayed a rather long prayer of thanks for the season and asked that God bless Mama with good health. He fixed his plate and turned to Elizabeth. "What did you learn in church today, Elizabeth?"

"Well, Papa, I learned that Jesus died in April." Very pleased with her vast knowledge of the Scripture, she leaned back in her chair.

"Now how do you know it was in April, Elizabeth?"

"Well, Papa, you told us the Passover was in the first month, which was April in the Jewish calendar, and preacher Grafton said they celebrated the Passover sure enough."

"So I did." He turned to Anna, and she knew that Papa's next question was for her. She had a little time to think of an answer to the question, and she wanted to have an answer as wonderful as her sister's. "Tell me what you learned, Anna."

Anna sat up very straight in her chair with the same confidence that Elizabeth had showed. "I learned that Jesus died for me, and that means that He loves me, and He was born in April, too." Papa smiled. He would have to discuss the possibility of Anna's last statement at a later date, when they had more time.

Elizabeth asked if she could discuss something that was on her mind. "Of course," Papa said. "Sounds serious."

After lunch, Elizabeth and Anna went with Papa into the west room. It seemed that things were "smarter" in there, according to Anna. "Well, my intelligent darlings, what would you like to discuss?"

Elizabeth began, "Papa, you know how Grandpa built this house for us and then named it Tehvah? Well, we always thought that it was just another name for a house. We want to know what Tehvah means."

"Elizabeth, that's a good question. I had forgotten about the time I had to ask your grandpa the very same question. You wouldn't know unless you could speak Hebrew."

"Well, Papa, we don't speak no Hebrew," Anna replied.

"You don't speak *any* Hebrew," corrected her father.

"Well, Papa, that's what I just said."

"So you did, but to answer your original question, Tehvah is the Hebrew word for *ark*. I suppose Grandpa believed that God wanted him to build an ark of sorts for his family like Noah built before the flood. You do know that it is just symbolic of God's watch care over us."

"Oh yes, if things get real bad, we can always run to the pea patch." Elizabeth smiled.

That night, after supper, there was a knock at the back door. Izzy was startled, because no one came to the back door after supper time. When Izzy went to the door, Zeb was standing there, cleaned up and with his hat in hand. "Miss Izzy, I wish to see Miss Simmy, if you please."

"Don't mind iffin you just set on the porch steps." Izzy called Simmy, who was listening from behind the door in her room. She was so excited that she needed a moment to calm down before she stepped out onto the porch.

Izzy never left the kitchen while Simmy and Zeb were on the back porch. She took in all the conversation, which wasn't much. Yet Izzy knew that her little girl had grown into a woman, and it wouldn't be long before Simmy would be married and leave Izzy alone. How she missed Isaac in her later years. *I sure wish he'd see our baby all growed up.* She thought of Isaac often, but never so much as she had lately. Simmy came inside with her head in the clouds and singing the praises of Zeb.

Elizabeth and Anna came running into the kitchen to say good night to Izzy and Simmy, but mostly because they had been spying when Zeb came to call. They wanted to know how Simmy felt about Zeb and if they would be losing a playmate and friend to marriage. Mama had already told them that Simmy was growing up and would want a family of her own before long.

Chapter 4

The year was flying by quickly, and Flora wondered if her child would ever come. She had not had any unsettling times during her pregnancy, but there had not been much movement from the baby in a few weeks.

It was a bleak November night when Flora knew that the time was near. As she began to feel the first subtle signs of labor, she was more relieved than worried. She was not concerned, because she had been through this before. Her husband would sleep for another hour before he climbed out of the cozy, warm bed piled high with the quilts that Flora and Grandma Effie had so carefully made. She laid there as quietly as she could so that she would not disturb her husband and prayed silently for a healthy baby as she waited for her contractions to come closer together and become more severe. She tried to occupy her mind with other things as she recalled the hours that Grandma Effie and she had spent making the quilts they now enjoyed so much. *I must have George get the quilting frames down from the attic later so that I can teach the girls how to quilt.* She thought of the time George had asked her to be his bride, how handsome he had been that day, and how she had loved him from the time she had first looked into those smiling eyes. She remembered Elizabeth's birth, with Izzy assisting Dr. Buie with the delivery. It was the same with Anna, and both deliveries went very well. *No need to expect anything different with this one,* she thought, and then she put those thoughts to rest.

Thankfully, George stirred a little earlier than usual, and Flora told him that the baby was on the way. He sprang to his feet, pulling on his clothes almost in the same motion. He called for Izzy so loudly that Flora's heart leapt a little. It was very uncharacteristic of George to raise his voice, especially to that level. *He must still be half asleep*, Flora thought.

Izzy had heard the alarm come from upstairs. "That baby's on the way!" she exclaimed as she fairly jumped into her work dress. She ran into the kitchen and stoked the coals in the big wood-burning stove until she saw the little flame lap the charred half of the burned wood that rested inside. Placing new, dry wood carefully over the flames, Izzy mumbled to herself. "Oh, Lord, don't nobody else know that you gotta have water to birth a li'l baby? I declare, they needs to learn 'fore any more chillen try and come into this world." She added more wood. "That baby be blessed to have old Izzy for its mammy." Izzy was not unkind; this was simply her way of releasing tension. Everyone in Tehvah knew to just get out of Izzy's way when they heard her babbling.

A large pot of fresh-pumped water was set on top of the stove to boil. Izzy retrieved clean, white cloths from the cupboard, which she had prepared earlier for this special event. Since she had helped deliver Elizabeth and Anna and even George without much assistance from old Dr. Buie, she felt confident in her ability. There was always apprehension about something going wrong, and this nagging thought came to her as she prayed aloud, "Oh, Lord, help me recall all I's s'posed to do."

The morning sun climbed higher in the sky, and Flora knew that it would not be long till they would welcome their precious little one into their lives. By this time, Simmy had told Elizabeth and Anna about the baby, and the three went into the parlor to sit and wait for the baby to arrive.

"*Humph.* I ain't never havin' no chillen," Simmy remarked. Her eyes widened as she listened to Flora Torrey's cry of considerable discomfort. "They's truouble 'fore they gets here and trouble after they be here 'fore quite a while." She felt quite philosophical after such a profound statement. Simmy felt that she could make such statements, especially after listening to Mr. George explain some perplexing problem she was facing. Most of these problems involved Izzy, true enough, but she could always find an answer when she talked with Mr. George.

"Is Mama all right, Elizabeth?" Anna's voice showed her concern.

Feeling very knowledgeable on the subject of giving birth and having seen some of the animals give birth, Elizabeth answered her little sister. "Mama will be just fine as soon as the baby comes out."

Anna's face showed her puzzlement over her sister's answer. "Out from where, Elizabeth?"

Elizabeth knew that she would really have to don her "smart cap" to tackle this one. "Well, Anna, didn't you see our pig have babies last spring?"

"No." Simmy wondered where the wizard would go with her explanation now.

"Well, what do you suppose that belly button is for?"

"That don't make any sense to me, Elizabeth. How could a baby get out that way?"

"Anna, it's just like the Bible story of the camel going through the eye of the needle. It's a miracle!" Simmy just shook her head. Elizabeth, impressed by what might be the best tale she had ever told, sat back and watched Anna's open mouth as she tried in vain to visualize the miracle of birth.

Miss Lizbeth needs to be shamed of such a tale, Simmy thought. *Iffin' she truly believe what she done told, she in for a whoppin' surprise.*

Suddenly, a baby's cry was heard from the downstairs bedroom, where Mama was. Anna smiled. "Mama is just fine now."

"Anna." Elizabeth spoke to Anna in hushed tones. "Since Mama already knows about birthing babies and how it goes, we really don't have to bring it up in our conversation."

Simmy tucked her chin down to her chest and smiled. "I just bet you don't want to bring up that li'l talk you just had with your li'l sister. That'd mean some trouble for one Miss Lizbeth."

The girls rushed to the door of the bedroom and waited for Papa's okay to come inside. Papa gave them a nod but stayed between the girls and the bed. Izzy had already cut the cord and tied it with a silk thread. She was cleaning the baby with soft, warm cloths.

"Well, Izzy, tell us what we have."

Tears were streaming down her face as she held up the red, screaming infant. "He be a boy, Mr. George. You got yourself a son." The child was small but had a very healthy set of lungs. Izzy handed little Hugh to his mother, and Flora placed her little son on her breast.

Papa herded the girls back into the parlor, where they sat down. Elizabeth, now regretting educating Anna on the birth process, thought it wise to begin the conversation before Anna could tell Papa what she had learned today.

"When can we see him and hold him?" Elizabeth was very excited and nervous at the same time. "Can we name him? Let's call him a dignified name, like Zachariah."

"Oh, Elizabeth, he could never learn to spell that. You might just as well call him Ecclesiastes." Anna was not really too excited about naming the baby, anyway. Simmy voted to call him Zebulon after Zeb.

"Those are all really good names, but Mama and I decided when we knew that we would have this baby that we would name him Hugh Webster Torrey. These are family names. Your grandpa Torrey had brothers named Hugh and Webster."

"What would that make us?" Anna asked.

"That's an interesting story," George answered. "That would make them your great-uncles, but the best part comes on down the line. Your Grandpa Torrey and his brother, Hugh, married two sisters—your Grandma Effie and her sister, Elizabeth. That meant that any children they had would be double first cousins."

"That hurts my head," said Anna.

Papa smiled. "Don't worry about it now. You can understand it better later."

"Do you think we can see him now, Papa? I sure would like to hold him." Elizabeth was on her feet.

Anna jumped to her feet. "I ain't even had my breakfast."

"Why, Anna Jane, ants are insects that crawl on the ground." Elizabeth felt a return to her vast knowledge of life and the creatures of the universe. "And most likely, they have already carried off your breakfast."

Mr. George need to have a li'l talk with Miss Smarty Pants, Simmy thought as they sat down once again, waiting to see the baby. Elizabeth silently thanked the Lord for Hugh Webster and for not letting Anna spill the beans about their little birthing discussion. Anna's prayer was somewhat different, as she prayed that God would miraculously put that baby back without any harm to Mama. There was much walking on tippy toes when little Hugh was sleeping. Anna thought the baby got far more attention than he deserved. Simmy would sometimes forego her play with Elizabeth and Anna for a chance to mind little Hugh. This fact did not sit well with Anna, who had formed quite a bond with Simmy. There was also the time Simmy spent with Zeb as they talked about marriage and moving into one of the small cottages to begin their lives together. Anna felt alone and forgotten except by Papa, her knight in shining armor. He seemed to always know what she was feeling and rescue her from any dire situation.

There was unease in the South during this time, but the true impact of the times had not come to the little community of Scotland.

Izzy was getting on up in years and had to depend more and more on Simmy to help with the cooking and enlist the help of another lady who lived in the slave quarters to help with the cleaning inside the main house. The new lady's name was Ruth, and she had come with her husband, Jim, from the North Carolina area. She had taught Simmy some of the Gullah language spoken by her parents. This made Simmy feel an instant kinship with Ruth. Gullah was a pidgin spoken by the slaves from that region. This was called the language of Sea Island.

When Simmy first approached Ruth about enlisting her help, Ruth asked, "Yo beliap?" Knowing that Simmy did not understand her Gullah, she continued, "Yo koolsik?"

"You knows I don't speak that mess." Embarrassed, Simmy began to walk away.

"Kambek," Ruth called, "and I tell you what I say. *Beliap* mean belly-up or you on your back in trouble. *Koolsik* mean you sick with cold; *kambek* mean come back. You don't know 'cause we speak language of Sea Island. I can teach you." Simmy soon began to catch on to the Jamaican sound of the words and didn't feel so ignorant about Gullah.

As the days went by, Izzy had less to do and spent most of her day mending clothes, gathering eggs, and even doing a bit of fishing in the little creek behind the main house. She did not like new people messing with her kitchen, but she soon realized that she could not do the work that she had done in the past. She spent hours near the oak tree meeting place, which was situated just in front of the grave of her dear Isaac and of Simmy's mother. She talked to both of them about Simmy, the Torreys, the crops, and anything else that was on her mind.

In the first week of December, the weather turned bitter cold, and the white snow came down heavily. The week was the coldest George could remember. It was unusual to see that much snow in Mississippi, but now it covered the fields, and ice formed around the edges of the little creek. The white smoke could be seen as it rose skyward from the chimneys on the cottages in the slave quarters.

When she looked out the kitchen window, Simmy could see an occasional white-tailed deer foraging around in the frozen garden for food. A rabbit hopped by, leaving deep tracks in the snow on the quest to find any vegetation that may have survived the freeze. "I s'pose it be too cool for folk to get out and kill any of them varmints. Sure be good eatin', though."

Simmy was making soup and corn bread for dinner from the canned vegetables stored in the pantry. "Let's see; 'maters, okra, pole beans, taters, and onions from the bin." It would be good to have hot soup for Izzy, who did not feel well.

That night, Izzy's cough was deep and hard. Flora came in to see what she could do to help while Simmy waited beside Izzy's bed, ready to spring into action at a moment's notice. She felt helpless as she sat by her mother's side. Flora bathed Izzy's face with cool water as George came into the room. "She has a fever, George. I think you may need to go and fetch Dr. Buie now."

Simmy fell on her knees at the bedside of the only mother she had ever known and prayed silently, *Oh, Lord, please don't take my Izzy; she all I got.*

George put on his heaviest coat, hat, and gloves. He went to the barn, where Zeb already had the horse hooked to the buggy. "How Miss Izzy doin', Mr. George?" he asked with genuine concern in his voice.

"Not too well, I'm afraid—but Zeb, I'm worried about Simmy. You may need to go inside and give her some support. You know that when Izzy is gone, she will feel all alone."

"But I won't let her be, Mr. George." Zeb made his way through the blowing, icy snow for Tehvah and Simmy.

George climbed into the buggy and headed for town. In the buggy, snow stung George's face. The horse raced through the untraveled little road, the buggy bouncing as the wheels broke through icy ruts made by buggies earlier in the season. George reached the closed office of Dr. Buie and headed immediately for his home. The small plantation-style home of Dr. Buie looked inviting. The warm glow of lamps shined through the windows and onto the snow.

George went up to the door and knocked. Dr. Buie opened the door hurriedly, sensing that there must be someone who was mighty sick.

"George, is it the baby?"

"No, Doc, it's Izzy. Flora thinks it might be pneumonia. Can you come with me?"

"Of course, George. I'll just get my bag and a few things in case I have to stay through the night."

"Thank you, Doc. I sure do appreciate it."

"Well, you know how I feel about Izzy."

Dr. Buie gathered his things quickly, and the two started back toward Tehvah. Dr. Buie was a kind man, and on this night, in his heavy coat, with his white beard and hair, under the cover of darkness, he might have passed for Santa. If he had anything in that black bag that could make Izzy well, they would all call him Santa.

Zeb heard the arrival of the horse and buggy, grabbed his coat, and ran out to the barn to unhitch the horse and put the buggy away. George was very grateful to see him and rushed Dr. Buie into Izzy's room. Flora was beside her bed, still bathing Izzy's head and looking very concerned. Simmy was back on her knees by the bed, cradling her head in her hands, half praying and half silently weeping.

Dr. Buie thought it best to give Simmy something to do. "Simmy, would you fill a big pot of water so that it can boil on the stove? The steam in the air will help your mama with her breathing."

As Simmy rose from her knees to help, Zeb came back into the room and moved to help Simmy with the water. She and Zeb went to the kitchen to fill the pot. It was clear that Simmy was much calmer with Zeb around.

Dr. Buie listened first to Izzy's rattling chest and knew beyond reason that it was pneumonia. The quinine came out of his little black bag along with a jar of camphor to help with her breathing. "I'll stay till I see some improvement, if that's all right with you, Flora."

"Of course, Doctor. We appreciate it so much. We want our Izzy to get well."

By morning, there was some improvement in Izzy's condition, but she was still very weak. The dark night had turned into a brand new day. The sun came up, its light glistening across the snow like diamonds in the sun.

Elizabeth and Anna had fallen asleep in the parlor in the overstuffed chair beside the fireplace. Ruth had come from her cottage to fix breakfast for the weary crew. The smell of fresh-brewed coffee on the stove seemed to put new life back into the old doctor.

Telling Simmy that she could cook the breakfast alone seemed the thing to do, and Ruth took on the role of being her helper. Simmy had not realized how hungry she was until she started to fry the bacon and eggs. Ruth sliced some bread she had made the day before and set out the dishes. The coffee was poured, and the girls came in from the parlor, anxious to hear about Izzy. The lack of news led them quietly to the breakfast table, where they prayed and ate in silence.

After breakfast, Elizabeth and Anna walked by the door of Izzy's room. The smell of camphor and the sound of Izzy's labored breathing were unavoidable. Little Hugh's cry sent Flora from the room for the morning feeding. It seemed like just another day except for their beloved Izzy's condition. Outside, the wind howled around the house, and the snow continued to blow in from the north. Elizabeth watched the snow from her bedroom window with Anna.

"The north wind doth blow, and it shall be cold. What will the robin do then, poor thing?"

"Is that from the Bible, Elizabeth?"

"No, silly, it's from me."

Dr. Buie called George into the west room for a talk. "George, Izzy's condition has improved, but she is very weak, and the thing that bothers me the most is that Izzy seems to have no fight left—no will to live. If that doesn't change, I'm afraid no medicine on the face of this earth will help."

"Maybe I can talk to her."

"I think that would be a good idea, George."

Dr. Buie left for town with Zeb in the buggy. There would be a lot of sick folks needing his help. He would have a busy night ahead, and he had done all he could do for Izzy.

Back at Tehvah, George went into Izzy's room. "Izzy, may I come in for a minute and talk with you? You don't have to talk if you don't want to." Izzy nodded. "Dr. Buie says that you seem to be giving up, even though there has been improvement in your sickness."

Izzy held up her shaky hand from her bed, and George strained to hear every word. "Mr. George," she began in the softest tones, "I just so tired. I's ready to go and be with Jesus. I wants to see my Isaac and all my kinfolk. I wants you to talk to Simmy and tell her to let me go. I's ready, and I wants to go home."

George did not have an argument for Izzy's decision—not one that would stand up in any court in heaven or on earth. "God bless you in your decision, Izzy. We will surely miss you." George walked to Izzy's bed and kissed her cheek. He knew that he would never see her again on earth.

That night, Izzy slipped over to her promised land. She was buried in the cemetery between her beloved Isaac and Simmy's mother. In her lifetime at Tehvah, she had been there to deliver George, Elizabeth, Anna, and Hugh. She had cared for Grandma Effie when she became ill and anyone who was in need of care. Now her labors were over, and she was at rest. Izzy's funeral was a celebration of her life. People bundled up, black and white alike, and filled the grounds behind Tehvah to honor Izzy's life.

"Amazing Grace" rang out across the snow in beautiful four-part harmony. The words of an old spiritual would begin with a beautiful, single voice and then be picked up by another and another until a whole choir of people sang the song of praise. There were tears, of course, but the thing that Elizabeth and Anna would remember most in the years to come would be how the people sang. Oh, how they sang!

Izzy died exactly one month after Hugh was born, and Elizabeth thought how sad it was for Hugh that he would never get to know her Izzy.

Chapter 5

It was almost Christmas time, and it was painful to think of decorating the house, since Izzy had just died. Flora thought it might help to take the children's minds off losing Izzy if they could concentrate on something else. She talked to George about taking the little sled into the woods to cut a tall Christmas tree for the parlor. George got his axe and the sled and called the girls. It was still very cold, but Elizabeth and Anna bundled up in warm coats, hats, mittens, and scarves. To their delight, Simmy and Zeb were going along to help.

The snow crunched under their feet. As they headed to the woods, the sled left little tracks in the snow. The bright sunshine had melted the top of the snow a little, and it formed a crust as the cold wind blew across it again. Just inside the woods that ran beside the cotton field, a big buck snorted at them and scampered deeper into the under growth. Anna stopped her forward movement. "What in the world was that?"

"Oh, Anna, it's just a deer looking for food. You've seen them before." Elizabeth was a bit put out by Anna's skittishness. "After all, this *is* where they live."

My goodness, Anna thought. She really didn't like the idea of sharing the woods with something that big.

"Oh, I see one," Elizabeth cried, frosty vapor escaping from her mouth. It was a tall, perfectly shaped cedar with nice, heavy branches that held up pounds of snow. Everyone agreed on the tree, and Papa took his axe and made short work of the chopping. Papa and Zeb dragged it to the sled. It was much longer than the sled, but they placed it so that the trunk extended over the back. That way, none of the limbs would be broken on the ride home.

Five days before Christmas, George returned from a meeting at the little community church with some disturbing news. They had received a message by telegraph that South Carolina had seceded from the Union.

"What does this mean, George?" Flora was quite concerned but did not fully understand the gravity of the situation.

"Right now, it means that more slave-holding states will do the same thing."

"This can't be good," she continued.

"We won't worry about it yet," said George. "We don't want to borrow trouble."

The very next day, they received word that Mississippi had fallen in line with South Carolina and seceded from the Union. Around the governor's mansion in Jackson, people gathered to discuss the rapid secession of Florida, Alabama, Georgia, and Louisiana. The state of Texas would not secede until the first day of February. Jefferson Davis had represented Mississippi in the United States Senate but would come home to Mississippi and be made President of the Confederate States of America.

That evening, George thought it wise to keep to the regular routine of the family. He took down the shorter catechism from the mantel and turned to the question about the Ten Commandments. It was difficult, and Elizabeth told her papa that she needed more time to study. Anna slipped into the parlor after her father had left, not having been a witness to her sister's inability to answer Papa's question. Anna noticed the pained expression on her sister's face and asked, "What's wrong with you, Elizabeth?"

"I'm gonna write my own catechism, and it won't be so hard."

"Yeah, Papa might really like that. You already know that Jesus was born in April."

At the supper table that night, Anna asked if she might return thanks. Looking very pleased with his young daughter, Papa nodded his approval.

Anna began, "Dear Lord, thank you for your mercies, for our food, and for our family; and Lord, please help Elizabeth to write a really good catechism. In Jesus' name. Amen."

Anna raised her head and looked for approval in Papa's eyes. He smiled down at Anna but decided not to tackle that last prayer request until he had some idea what it meant.

The next morning, the family heard carriage wheels in the rocks on the front path. Anna peered out her upstairs window to see that their guest was Mr. McEachern, an elder from the church. He was an older, pious-looking man with beautiful white hair, like Dr. Buie's. As he stepped down from the buggy to the ground, the buggy sprang back up a considerable way. Anna thought it was plain to see that his garden had done quite well that year.

Papa went out to meet him. Elizabeth joined Anna at the window, and as was their custom, raised the window very quietly in order to hear the conversation. The men spoke in low tones.

"What'd he say?" Anna was anxious to know why Mr. McEachern would make a special trip to Tehvah, especially when it was not an occasion where food was being served.

"Hush, Anna, I can't hear what he's saying with you yapping in my ear."

Anna fell quiet, and after a short while, Elizabeth pulled her head inside and eased the window down.

"Well, all I could hear was something about a meeting at the church this afternoon to pray about our dilemma, whatever that is."

"Oh, no. Elizabeth, do you remember last summer when we needed rain for the crops? We went to the church, and Mr. McEachern prayed for rain. He prayed and prayed and prayed. He prayed for so long that when we got into the buggy to go home, the rain started to come down. It rained so hard that I thought we would drown before we could get home. Papa said that he thought Mr. McEachern may have prayed a little too long!"

"Yeah, I remember it really was a frog-strangler. No telling what will happen if he prays that long for our dilemma."

At the church meeting that afternoon, there was talk of the states seceding from the Union, as expected.

"If our brothers in North Carolina, Tennessee, and Arkansas decide on this same course, there may be conflict," Mr. McEachern concluded.

"I'm sure glad he didn't decide to pray about it," Anna whispered to Elizabeth, relieved. "We'd probably be here till next Christmas."

By the first of February, six states had joined the southern cause and left the Union. Eventually, there would be thirteen. In April, there was still one fort in South Carolina that was manned by federal troops. It was located in Charleston Harbor, and the supplies were sufficient to last only a couple weeks more. The troops were few in number; thus, Lincoln decided to send supplies and more troops into South Carolina.

A bloody conflict would begin here when shots were fired on federal forces. Men rushed to enlist in the conflict, which would accelerate quickly into a bloody civil war.

Abraham Lincoln was inaugurated as President of the United States of America on March 4. Jefferson Davis was President of the Confederate States with Alexander Stephens of Georgia as his Vice President. The war had begun—North against South, each side with conflicting ideas of why they were about to kill each other. Each believed it was right. For the people in the North, the conflict was about slavery, and in the South, it was about keeping land and property.

George went to the west room retreat to pray for guidance on the path he should take. This was not totally unexpected, considering all the animosity toward the southern way of life in recent years. He had read a book by Harriet Beacher Stowe entitled *Uncle Tom's Cabin*. Although she had never lived a day in the South, her book extolled the cruelty of slavery. He could not deny that some slave owners were cruel to their slaves, but among George's acquaintances, slaves were treated with love and respect. George had freed the slaves purchased by his father years ago because of his own personal conviction. Most had chosen to stay with him and live as free men, because they were cared for and treated well. Some left for the unknown, and only six of the original twelve cottages were now occupied.

Simmy, of course, still lived in the main house. Although George believed the Bible made allowances for having slaves, he did not align himself with their mistreatment or their sale and purchase, as his father had. He also knew that he would have to take a stand for his family and his land. Most of the men who volunteered to fight did not own slaves. They were poor white farmers who worked their own land and felt obligated to fight in defense of their Southland. The Fugitive Slave Law of 1850 stirred up much opposition in the North and put them on the road to all-out war.

In the days ahead, it became increasingly harder for George to keep his family going with only a small crew of laborers. This made it impossible to enlist—or was this just an excuse for not becoming involved in something that might require him to take another man's life? He could not truly say, but he kept up with the war via the newspaper out of Jackson and the telegraph in town.

In mid-July of 1861, news came about a battle of Manassas near Washington. About thirty-five thousand Union soldiers, under the command of General Irvin McDowell, left Washington. Having never witnessed a battle and fearing no danger, a great audience of civilians rode in buggies and on horses to see the route of the arrogant Johnny Rebs. Women with parasols and picnic lunches sat on a ridge overlooking the proposed site of the battle. They sang choruses of "Rally Round the Flag, Boys," and the men chanted, "On to Richmond!" This serene gathering of onlookers would soon turn to chaos.

General Pierre G. T. Beauregard commanded the main body of around twenty thousand Confederates. His orders were to protect the railroad junction as well as cut off the route to Richmond. On that evening of the July 17, Beauregard positioned some of his troops along the bank of Bull Run facing Washington; some protected the railroad junction while the rest were at a bridge where the federal troops were approaching. About three or four miles from the bridge, one division advanced to test the rebel line and were sent packing. They retreated to Centerville to plan their main attack and enlist the use of their reserve troops. They intended to outnumber the rebel forces. They had underestimated the unflinching spirit of the southerners.

Meanwhile, reinforcements came from the Shenandoah Valley, led by Stonewall Jackson, Jeb Stuart, and Joe Johnston. When Johnston's men were told that they were marching to aid Beauregard at Manassas, a mighty shout went up from every man—the very first rebel yell of this difficult and bloody war.

The news came by telegraph to Jackson. On the steps of the capitol, the familiar strains of "Dixie" were offered up by enthusiastic old statesmen. The report of casualties for the first battle came over the telegraph. Of the Virginia brigade, only 112 were killed and 393 wounded. The federal army had suffered a total loss of about three thousand killed, wounded, or missing. The total number of Confederates was about two thousand. It was at this first Manassas that Thomas Jackson of West Virginia, a graduate of West Point, earned his nickname of "Stonewall." In the second round at Manassas, with their ammunition gone, his men fought with stones.

Back at Tehvah, the girls went back to the creek, their pockets filled with stones, and they terrorized the turtles with renewed vigor. "Take that, you Billy Yank," Elizabeth shouted as she hurled her rocks in earnest. Anna and Simmy responded with a rousing rebel yell.

Zeb enlisted in the army, as many of the slaves had done. Some were pressed into service, but Zeb felt that since he and Simmy would soon be jumping the broom and making their own home, he must defend his South against her enemies.

"He be handsome in that raggedy li'l grey suit an li'l hat set all crooked on his head." Simmy spoke proudly of Zeb. "When they's through whoopin' them Billy Yanks, he gonna come home, and we's gonna jump the broom."

Elizabeth and Anna became weary of hearing about Zeb and Simmy's matrimonial plans and began a second Manassas on the hapless turtles in the little creek. *"Yee-awee!"* shouted both girls as they headed back to the creek and left Simmy to her dreaming.

Oh, Zeb, Simmy thought after the girls went back to battle, *ain't no use in all this yelling and killing and dying.* Simmy could imagine her Zeb running across the battlefield—and for what, she did not know.

Southerners sang the praises of Stonewall Jackson and his men for their bravery on the battlefield.

"Papa says General Jackson is a praying Presbyterian, just like us," Elizabeth said proudly.

"I'm glad," Anna answered, "but if he prays as long as Mr. McEachern does, he won't ever get any fighting done."

Chapter 6

April came, and the weather got warmer. The garden had to be planted. Papa worked until he got it done; however, it was considerably smaller than last year. He was bone-weary but climbed into the buggy for his daily trip down town for news on the fighting. A photographer named Matthew Brady had made it his mission to show the war with graphic pictures of the death and destruction caused by the battles.

In the coastal region, Brigadier General Ambrose Burnside entered inland waters of the North Carolina sound and captured Roanoke Island, Elizabeth City, and Edenton. By April 11, Fort Pulaski surrendered to federal forces, but the worst blow during this time was the South's loss of her principle port of New Orleans.

The Confederate ironclad *Merrimac* moved out of harbor in Norfolk, attacking the Union fleet and sinking the frigates *Cumberland* and *Congress*. The arrival of the Union ironclad *Monitor* avoided any further destruction by running down the *Merrimac* and destroying it in the harbor.

"It sounds as though we are being surrounded on all sides by Union forces," Dr. Buie went on. "Seems like after Nashville surrendered, things have been going poorly for us."

"I know we have all had relatives in the thick of the fighting in North Carolina as well as fatalities at the battle of Manassas," Reverend Grafton added.

Names were funny things at times. In the South, the battles were named for towns, and the North named battles for streams; hence, the South's battle at Manassas became the North's battle of Bull Run. It could be confusing depending on who you were discussing the war with.

As George listened to the discussions of the war in town, a feeling of guilt swept over him. He had not enlisted in defense of his homeland. In his heart, he could not truly say that he could kill another human being. He pondered what a unique commitment to a cause it must take to look another man in the eye and take his life. He took a moment to look through the names of the dead and wounded in search of any that he might recognize. Finding none, he went to his buggy and began his short trip back to Tehvah and the warm safety of his family.

Life had not been easy at Tehvah, but strong faith kept the family when things seemed to get worse with the crops, loss of laborers, and in general, the way the world seemed to be going.

Early shattering events would affect the Torreys. Born the year before the Civil War, Hugh had died. Dr. Buie could not explain the sudden death. It was as though he just fell asleep and did not wake up. Mama was deeply depressed but Papa accepted it as God's providence. Perhaps the most disturbed with Hugh's death was Anna.

As Anna gazed silently down at the shiny, golden curls and closed eyes of beautiful clear blue, she felt like her soul was in the darkest night. There was the slightest hint of a sweet smile on her little brother's face. No one but Anna and God knew of the childish prayer she had prayed when she asked God to take that baby back. How awful could she be? She burst into tears and ran from the parlor where Hugh lay in his tiny white coffin. She thought that if it were possible, she would trade places with him, and the world would be a better place.

She ran down the steps in back of the kitchen to the oak tree where she and Elizabeth had played so many times. How on earth could she be forgiven for such an awful sin? She prayed most earnestly for forgiveness, but never for one minute did she feel she deserved any kind of mercy.

Little Hugh would remain at home and be buried in the family cemetery beside Grandma, Grandpa, and the twins. Anna's heart had never ached so, and she could not even share her pain with Papa; she was too ashamed. At that moment, she recalled a verse of Scripture that spoke to her heart. "Cast your burdens upon the Lord for He cares for you."

The funeral ended, and the finality set in for all the family, but Anna would spend many long hours out back, sitting by the wrought iron gate, thinking about her little brother, who was resting safe with Jesus.

Chapter 7

George struggled through the year, but it was finally over—and with it, George hoped his struggles would be also. With the railroads transporting such great numbers of troops, he knew that the time would soon come when his home and his family would feel the effects of the war. Up in Chancellorsville, Lee had defeated Hooker at the great cost of losing Stonewall Jackson. General Lee was said to have remarked, "I have lost my right arm." To add to the devastating sadness of losing this brave man of prayer, Jackson was accidentally shot and killed by friendly fire. The federal troops had finally reached Mississippi. It was said that Yankee morale was low as the soldiers floundered aimlessly in the mud of Mississippi. Many were homesick and bedeviled by disease and pesky mosquitos. This news proved to be of little comfort to the rebel troops when they heard of Grant's march down the west bank of the Mississippi. There Grant's army defeated the outnumbered Confederate forces at Port Gibson. This position was alarmingly close to the little community of Scotland.

Back at Tehvah, Elizabeth and Anna still continued their systematic bombardment of the Yankee turtles. Flora sometimes worried that this practice might not be healthy for them, but Papa didn't seem to be too concerned.

Simmy felt that Zeb must surely be seeing action with the Yankees all around, but she had no idea in what part of the state he was deployed. Fortunately, the war had not physically touched their small community.

On May 12, Grant—with twenty thousand men—defeated Brigadier General John Gregg at the battle of Raymond and marched back to Jackson. Two days after the battle at Raymond, he captured the state's capitol. Next was the battle of Champion Hill very near to Clinton, a prosperous little town. Mississippi College was located there along with many fine antebellum homes owned by wealthy planters. Still, Tehvah saw no troops, but George felt that from the back-and-forth movement of his troops, Grant was headed for Vicksburg.

"Where do you think Zeb is now, George?" Flora was concerned, because they had no word on Zeb.

George frowed, "I really don't know, Flora, but I check on his name in the paper every day and pray for his safe return to us. I don't think Simmy could stand to lose him right now."

Simmy was now twenty-one years old and was beginning to think she would die an old maid. Elizabeth had grown taller and was eleven, while Anna was a girlie eight. Both had learned at least one catechism, and Elizabeth felt twice as smart as she was when she was ten.

"We got to find something else to do besides kill Yankee turtles," said Anna. "I figured that these turtles are not even from up north anyway."

"If we knew what to put in them," replied Elizabeth, "we could make tea cakes like Izzy used to make for us."

"I doubt if she knows, but we can ask Simmy."

They found Simmy sitting beside the little cemetery where her mother and Izzy were buried. She looked as though she was talking to someone.

"See, Elizabeth, I told you we could talk to Grandma and Grandpa Torrey."

"I didn't say you couldn't talk to them, Anna, but who knows if they hear you."

"God does," Anna answered as though Papa had asked a question from the catechism.

Papa was correct in his assumption that General Grant was headed for Vicksburg. Grant, along with about forty thousand men, had Vicksburg under siege. They couldn't penetrate the defenses without considerable losses, so the plan was to wait them out. Grant had cut off all supplies going into Vicksburg, and the people were forced to eat their mules in order to survive.

Desperate for news of the Vicksburg siege, George had made another trip into town. He first stopped by to read the list of dead and wounded. As he ran his finger down the long list of casualties, he stopped at a familiar name. His heart ached when he saw that Zebulon was among the missing at the battle of Champion Hill on the Union's march toward Vicksburg. How could he ever tell Simmy? Not knowing Zeb's condition, George made arrangements to travel to Jackson in an effort to find out anything he could and at the same time avoid his capture by federal troops. The word was that Jackson had been burned, and nothing was left standing but chimneys from the burned-out buildings. The capitol itself and the governor's mansion were still standing.

The next day was July 4, and George heard that Vicksburg surrendered to Grant's forces. This might be the best time to look for Zeb. George left that afternoon, hoping to reach Jackson under the cover of darkness. As he listened to the sound of the horse clipping along the road, he prayed silently for Zeb's deliverance and that Zeb would be well enough to return to Tehvah with him. He did not allow himself to even imagine Zeb being dead.

It was just about dusk when George heard the clatter of another horse approaching. His heart began to pound as it drew nearer. The horse was pulling a wagon, and George relaxed a bit, as it did not appear to be a threat. As he pulled to one side of the narrow lane to let the wagon pass, George heard a familiar voice.

"Mr. George?" It was Zeb riding in the back of the wagon. George could not curb his emotions as he jumped from the buggy.

"Zeb, are you all right?"

"I is now, Mr. George. Ain't no Yankee musket ball gonna keep me 'way from home and my Simmy." George helped Zeb out of the back of the wagon, giving him a bear hug in the process. Zeb gave a little grunt of pain, and George noticed a bandage on his arm.

"I'm sorry, Zeb," George said, not realizing that Zeb was in pain.

"No more war for me; I's goin' home." Thanking his fellow comrade in arms, Zeb climbed carefully into the buggy beside George. On the ride home, Zeb related the story of how he was shot and escaped into the woods with another soldier. They stayed in the woods until they thought it safe to walk to the little road leading away from the fighting. Some men made it home because of their position at Champion Hill. One of these men retrieved his wagon and volunteered to take Zeb and his friend to their homes.

The homecoming was a sight to see as Simmy hugged and fussed over Zeb. "I don't s'pose you be goin' back any time soon," Simmy teased.

"No, ma'am. I's got me a weddin' to go to."

They immediately began to make plans for the wedding. The next day, Zeb and Simmy went to talk to Joshua about doing a real ceremony at Simmy's request. "I don't want to just jump the broom; I wants a li'l Bible-readin' goin' on, too."

Simmy and Zeb were married by Joshua the next week, Bible-readin' and all. Elizabeth and Anna wore their best Sunday dresses, and George gave the bride away. They were married out back under the spreading oak so Izzy and Simmy's mama would be close. Simmy said that this way, it was like having them at the wedding.

Simmy moved out of the main house and into the house of Zebulon. They were very happy, but Anna was the least happy with the arrangement. This really cut into her time with Simmy.

Zeb helped George as much as he could while his arm healed. They became fast friends and spent a great deal of time talking about the war and all the bloodshed. At times, the old guilt of not serving came back to haunt George. It was Zeb who comforted him, "Mr. George, you woulda got yourself killed. I knows you couldn't shoot anybody. What'd this whole family do without you to run this place?"

The next year, people could talk of nothing but Sherman's march through Georgia. Then in February of 1865, Sherman reached Columbia, South Carolina, and before the next day was over, the city was consumed in flames. It was told by Sherman's men that he drank too much. When word reached Lincoln, he said that if that was the case, he'd buy a barrel of liquor for each of his generals. Sherman seemed to be bent on making an example of South Carolina, which was the first state to secede from the Union.

On April 9, 1865, Robert E. Lee surrendered at Appomattox Court House, and the war was officially over.

"What we's gonna do now, Mr. George?" Zeb and George sat on the porch and discussed the situation.

George looked into his friend's eyes. "You know that you've always been free to go anywhere you like, Zeb."

"Well, Mammy and Pappy done gone on to be with Jesus, and I doubts Simmy'd go anyplace else. This been her home all her life—and mine, too."

"Zeb, if you decide to stay on and help me with Tehvah, we'll section off a little piece of land to belong to you and Simmy. That will give you a little place of your own to raise your family."

"Don't know how we'd pay you, Mr. George."

"Your helping me with the planting and the harvest would be payment enough. I plan on cutting down on the crops considerably."

The next day, five other workers came to George asking for the same consideration. This was an answer to George's prayers. He would have enough help to keep Tehvah operating; at the same time, he could give his field hands an opportunity to have a place to call their own. Things seemed to be falling into place after a long and very difficult time.

On April 14, only five days after the surrender of General Lee at Appomattox Court House, President Lincoln was shot at Ford's Theater. John Wilkes Booth, a Southern sympathizer, fired the deadly shot. Ironically, Andrew Johnson of Tennessee became President of the United States of America. Lincoln's dramatic death overshadowed his shortcomings and emphasized his best traits.

In the South, the news of Lincoln's death was cheered by those who had fought and by some who had waited for the return of loved ones who never came home. In the North, the fantastic rumor spread that Jefferson Davis had taken part in the plot to assassinate President Lincoln.

In 1866, the Ku Klux Klan was formed in the state of Tennessee. It was designed to terrorize blacks and keep them in submission. These hooded gangs rode through the countryside, burning property and occasionally killing those who offered resistance.

Zeb came to George one morning as they were leaving to do a little work on the grounds of Tehvah. "Mr. George, I's becomin' fearful for my family 'cause of this KKK folk ridin' and killin'."

"Zeb, I don't think that will last. They aren't active in our county. I don't think we have to worry. They won't come to Tehvah." Since the war, George had neglected his weekly obsession with the news and was caught off guard with stories about the clan.

"I hear of a place in Louisiana where they's killed two hundred of my people and pile they bodies up in the swamp for the snakes and gators to eat."

George was outraged and at the same time deeply saddened at man's cruelty to his fellow man. "How can such evil exist, Zeb? I have regretted these years not enlisting as a soldier in the war, but hearing this, I thank my God that I never did. I will promise you, Zeb, that if ever faced with such people, I will defend you with my life."

Zeb knew that George meant what he said. Zeb pulled his short statue up as tall as he could and looked into George's dark, sincere eyes. "I knows that, Mr. George, and I do the exact same for you." The two friends walked back to their homes, each wondering the reason for all this war and insanity. It was like a different time—a different world.

At home, concern overtook George's thoughts. He wondered about his relatives in Arkansas and how the war had affected them. It was time he wrote a letter to his double first cousins. No letters had reached them during the years of the war, and now he felt he would be able to contact them.

George seated himself in front of the big desk in the west room and began to write.

> Dear cousins, I take pen in hand to inquire as to your general well-being after the war. God was good to us in this part of Mississippi. The fighting was close, but we did not encounter any federal troops or hear the noise of battle, for that matter. I surmised that they felt a community of old, white Presbyterians was not a threat to them. I did not enlist in the war effort and have had pangs of guilt about this neglect of service until one of my friends and workers told me about the KKK. I pray that your field hands do not encounter such fiendish offenses.
>
> We had a rather difficult time at the close of the war. Flora took out the loom and the quilting frame, and we drank that awful coffee that Papa and Uncle Hugh taught us to make. I know you remember grinding that wasted rye and sweet potatoes. When we ran out of sugar, we'd use molasses and honey. I never thought we would use that old recipe. As you may well imagine, I truly do appreciate my coffee now. It seems so strange to me that it takes experiencing

the worst of something for us to really appreciate the things we have.

Tehvah is in bad need of paint but has no structural damage. We plan on giving her a new coat of paint before the onset of the winter months. Enough of the field hands stayed with me to get the majority of the work done; however, my crop area is much smaller. I thank God each day for His goodness. Jackson was burned so badly that they are calling it Chimneyville, and that is only about sixty-five miles from our little community of Scotland.

I would be amiss if I did not inquire as to the hunting in the Arkansas woods. I feel sure that the deer and turkeys are in no danger with you two hunting them.

Give Mae and Rankin our love and say that we hope to see you all in the near future.

I will wait eagerly to hear from you,

Your cousin,

George Edward Torrey

George sealed his letter to Arkansas and mailed it, hoping for a quick response. He returned to Tehvah and sat in the west room to recount old memories. He and his cousins had played together as small children. He recalled the China berry wars long before Tehvah was in her present state. They had visited during summer months and spent much of their time hunting bull frogs in the creek, never fearing the snakes. Long grapevines became whips, and cattails from the water were finely crafted swords. *Hmm,* thought George, *it's a wonder we didn't put out an eye or get bitten by a snake.* George leaned back in his chair, folded his hands across his chest, closed his eyes, and smiled.

Chapter 8

The letter arrived addressed to John Dougal Torrey, Scotland Community, Junction City, Arkansas. The tall, thin man took the letter in his hand and hurried to the back of the plantation home. "Neill," he shouted, "we got a letter from ol' George in Mississippi." He waved the letter over his head and came to rest at the pile of wood Neill had been chopping. Neill Torrey, the younger by two years, was almost a carbon copy of his Mississippi cousin, even down to the mustache. "What does ol' George have to say?" Setting the axe aside, Neill sat down on the chopping stump, waiting to hear the news from Mississippi.

John read the prized letter aloud while Neill listened intently. After finishing the letter, he held it out to Neill. "Is ol' George insultin' our huntin' skills?"

"Just yours, Neill."

"I didn't hear anybody complain the day them Yankee blue-bellies came charging up that hill," Neill replied as he closed one eye and peered down the length of his arm as if he held a rifle.

"It ain't your shootin' I'm talkin' about. It's your runnin' that got you into trouble." Even in their thirties, John and his brother still teased each other like they had when they were boys.

Neill had taken some grape shot in his thigh near the end of the war that left him with a slight limp. John and Neill had built modest homes on the same land. Their father, Hugh, lived with his son, John, till his death in 1830. Right up until the year of his death, he would go out in the morning and inspect the apple trees on the place. If the gardens had been planted, he would look for green-horned worms on the tomato plants and removed the suckers that sapped some of the plant's nutrition between the branches. He liked to stay active and feel useful. John would compare him to Moses: "His eyes are still sharp, and his mind is bright."

In addition to the apple orchard and garden, the Torreys raised pigs and chickens. They had two cows and a bull for which they were very thankful. They grew cotton and some rice. Their lives were much simpler than that of their Mississippi cousin. They did not own slaves but employed hired hands when needed to help with their meager crops until their boys were big enough to help.

John's boys, Angus and Will, were older and had a little more work experience. Because of the difference in age, they thought they should have a little more authority over their cousins, George, Richard, and John David. This assumption had a tendency to cause problems, but since the older boys were outnumbered by their cousins, it soon because a moot point. For the most part, they enjoyed one another's company and were more like brothers than cousins.

They loved the mountainous terrain of their Arkansas home and truly felt sorry for their flat land cousins in Mississippi. They could hunt turkey, deer, and even wild boars, although the wild boars were quite dangerous. Two of their hunting dogs had been wounded by the long tusks of these animals. They had decided to give up this particular type of hunting—not only because one of their dogs may be killed, but also because the meat tasted musky. There was also the problem of their mothers objecting. After all, they could go to the smokehouse and eat the pork they had raised on their own farm.

Neill's boys, George, Richard, and John David, enjoyed their own outings without Angus and Will. Besides being perfectly capable of taking care of themselves, they sometimes considered the older boys a bit bossy.

It was a nice, warm day in spring—the first warm day of the year. The younger boys were at the edge of the woods, looking for turkey tracks, deer, or anything they could hunt except wild boars. Richard was moving the leaves that were still on the ground from the winter when he disturbed a very unwelcome guest. Backing up slowly, as his father had told him to do, Richard announced, "There's a snake under these leaves!"

The snake was coiled up on the ground and ready for action. His skin was shiny and black as coal. "He's not poisonous," David said and took a step closer to the snake. There was a flash of black toward the movement as the snake struck at David's leg. Narrowly missing its target, the snake returned to the coiled position.

"Hey," George yelled as all three boys jumped back. For some reason, the snake became more aggressive and began to slither in their direction. With this totally unexpected move on the snake's part, the boys turned in the direction of home. They made a mad dash with the snake in hot pursuit.

"What is that thing?" Richard yelled as he ran at top speed.

"It's a coach whip," George replied, "and he's gaining on us."

David was out in front of the others, his knees almost hitting his chest, arms flying and fists pumping like pistons. Up the porch steps and through the back door he went. George and Richard heard the click of the heavy lock.

"Hey, he locked the door!" Richard screamed.

"Then run around the house," puffed George.

"David, open the door!" Richard yelled as he neared the back of the house. Not realizing that the snake had left the chase before they reached the house, the boys circled the house twice. On the third lap, David opened the door to admit his panting brothers.

Too exhausted to jump on his brother at that moment, Richard screamed, "Why did you lock the door, dummy? I can't believe you did that!"

"Well, I didn't want Mama fussing at us for letting a snake in the house."

Many days would pass before George and Richard would accept David's company again. There was much planning on retaliation for David's unholy act. For weeks afterward, David would carefully inspect his bed for frogs, snakes, or other foreign creatures before he climbed in at night.

The next week was even warmer, and the cousins invited a friend named Angus Kelly to join them on one of their excursions. His full name was Angus Gilchrist Kelly, and since one of the cousins was named Angus as well, they called him A. G. As the boys walked toward the creek, poles in hand, Angus turned to his friend.

"A. G., how come you got a Scottish first name and an Irish last name?"

A. G. looked a little annoyed with the question. "Oh, I'm Scottish, all right. Grandpa told me that a long time ago, my kinfolk were bodyguards in Ireland."

"What's that got to do with anything?"

"Well," A. G. continued, "he told me that some Scots hired the Kellys to bring over some Irish women to be brides for them, 'cause the Scottish women were so ugly."

"What?" Richard was slightly offended. "My mama is Scottish, and she ain't ugly. You need to take that back."

"You asked the question, and my mama is Scottish, too." A. G.'s red hair betrayed his Irish heritage, and secretly, he was a bit proud of it. It made him feel just a little more special living in this community of Scottish Presbyterians. Although his family had embraced this faith for hundreds of years, he often wondered what it would be like to be an honest-to-goodness wine-drinking Catholic. He would never know.

At the creek, the boys baited their hooks with worms they had dug and threw their lines into the water. "Some little blue gills would be a real good eatin'," A. G. said as he saw the cork on his line bob a little.

"I'm gettin' a bite!"

Richard became interested in A. G.'s line, "It's probably just a turtle or a little bitty fish sucking off your bait."

A. G. stood up from his stooped position and gave his pole a yank to set the hook.

A. G. was only fourteen, but he was strong, with long, muscular arms that had developed from hard work beside his father and brothers on their farm.

"Hold on, A. G.," David shouted. "Looks like a keeper to me." David was looking at the determination in the face of A. G. as he wrestled with the fish and knew at that moment that he wanted A. G. for a friend. The pole bent downward as A. G. pulled and snaked the fish on to the bank of the creek. Once on the bank, the boys all gathered to look at the fifteen-pound catfish.

"It's just an ol' mud cat," Angus chided. "Mama wouldn't even fool with cleanin' him."

Embarrassed by his cousin's attempt to minimize A. G.'s big catch, David interrupted, "You're just jealous, because you didn't catch him, Angus."

With a wink toward David, A. G. took the fish off the hook. "I guess you're right, Angus; I might as well just throw this old cat right back into the creek."

Realizing that he might miss out on a fine meal, Angus did a little bit of crawfishing. "No, wait a minute, A. G.; no need in doin' that. Besides, that'd be a waste of one of our biggest night crawlers."

"Yeah," replied David, "a real waste."

They all laughed as A. G. baited his hook with another prize night crawler. The fishing continued until it was almost lunchtime. A. G.'s big catfish was inside a large bucket with holes punched into the bottom. The bucket sat in the creek with a strong rope tied to the handle. When the boys were ready to go home, they retrieved the bucket, which now held five blue gill bream and a small white perch. None of them came close to the catfish that A. G. had landed. This would be the day A. G. established himself as a great fisherman.

Eyeing his fish with a great deal of pride, A. G. called out to Angus, "I bet some of them hungry boys in the war would have liked this big old fish a lot. Makes me want to break out with 'Dixie.'"

Richard became somber. "I heard the Yankees sing a song, too. You know what they're singing, don't you?" No answer came. "I'm gonna tell you. 'Hang Jeff Davis on a sour apple tree.' But President Johnson gave Jeff Davis a pardon. Now I guess they'll be hollerin' to hang President Johnson on a sour apple tree."

"I think Grandma is related to President Johnson, but she just won't admit it."

"I don't blame her," David continued. "It must be embarrassing to have to live up there in the middle of all them land-grabbin' Yankees. Down with the North! Wish we had another shot at 'em!"

"Oh, I wish I was in the land of cotton. Old times there are not forgotten. Look away, look away, look away, Dixie land."

"Yahoo!" A roaring yell rose into the sky from deep in the Arkansas hills, and six young boys strolled happily toward home with their precious cargo.

Chapter 9

The Arkansas hills were alive with the new growth that spring brings. The wildflowers were beginning to grow and would soon cover the hillsides. The old people compared it to the heather on the hills of Scotland. Grandma Johnson's family Bible had a little poem written at the bottom of the records page:

> From the lonely shieling of
> The misty island,
> Mountains divide us and a
> Waste of seas.
> Yet still the blood is strong
> The heart is Highland,
> And we in dreams behold
> The Hebrides.

There was a real love for the land that had never been visited or even seen by the boys. They had been taught from an early age to respect things that were dear to their family. Deep inside, there was hope that someday, they might go there to satisfy the longing in their hearts to go home. There would still be snow in the Hebrides but no heather visible on the hillsides. The weather would be cold, and boats would be in the safe harbor on the Isle of Skye in the Highlands. The Torreys were a sept of the clan Campbell, while the Kellys, A. G.'s family, were a sept of the clan Donald. Stories from both families had passed down from the time when the people spoke only Gaelic.

Although none of A. G.'s family spoke Gaelic, his grandma had made them all learn one phrase: *"Ni h-eibhneas gan Chlainn Domhnaill."*

"What's it mean, son?" Grandma Torrey asked.

"It means, 'It is no joy without clan Donald.'" He told her the story of the McDonalds arriving on the Isle of Skye in the fifteenth century from the southern Hebrides.

Grandma Torrey smiled as she remembered her own family's account of the story. "Did your grandma tell you about what happened at Glencoe?"

"Yes, ma'am." A. G. embarked upon the McDonald version of the "massacre" of the McDonalds as they slept one night on top of Signal Hill.

"According to Grandma, it was a dark night, and the Campbells slipped into the McDonald camp while they slept and murdered them. Seems the McDonalds had accused the Campbells of being cattle thieves, and they were looking for revenge. Grandma said the fight would have been much closer if the McDonalds hadn't been roaring drunk."

"That's more than likely pretty close to the way it happened." Grandma sat back in her chair, impressed with A. G.'s knowledge. The beauty of the whole thing was that the boys never even realized that at a different time and in a different place, their ancestors had been mortal enemies.

A. G., who was almost always with the brothers, told Grandma about a Gilchrist toast that his grandma shared with him.

"Do you remember it, Son?" Grandma asked.

"Yes, ma'am. 'Here's to the heath and the heather; the bonnet, the plaid, the kilt, and the feather. Here's to the heroes that Scotland can boast; may their names never die.' That's the clan Gilchrist toast."

"Well, that's a fine toast. You be sure to teach that to your children, Son." Grandma was a wealth of information. The boys were sure that she would remember that toast just in case A. G. forgot it.

It was time for the spring planting, and the boys' activities would be limited to working with John and Neill in the fields. They would come in bone-tired, but they looked on this as a duty to their parents for their care and protection over the years. There was no complaining on their part; helping with the work was just what they did.

The planting time was always long and hard, but when the work was done, there was a celebration. John and Neill would pull the two long wooden tables together in the area between their two houses and pray it didn't rain the next day. When the sun came up the next morning, Rankin and Mae were busy cooking for the big feast the two families would enjoy together.

Rankin had a ham from the smokehouse ready for the oven, and Mae killed two chickens for frying. The breakfast would not be elaborate on this morning because of all the cooking that had to be done for the early dinner.

Potatoes were bought from the cellar along with onions for a potato stew. Rankin would have to consult with Mae as to what canned vegetables she intended to cook so as not to repeat any dishes. Neither had any specialty dishes, because they were both very good cooks.

When Rankin went to her sister-in-law's house to see what vegetables she would prepare, she could smell apple pies baking in the oven. "How many pies did you make, Mae?"

"I'm baking three. Do you think that will be enough?"

"Well, let's see," Mae counted. "In my family, there are five, and in yours, there are six. That's eleven, and if A. G. comes—and I'm sure he will—there will be twelve."

"Three ought to be plenty. Besides, I'm making a buttermilk cake." Rankin felt they had desserts covered. She continued with the menu.

"I thought I would cook some beans and okra, because I still have jars and jars left from the winter."

"I need to use up some pickles and tomatoes. I'll come up with something using them and stuff some eggs." Mae wiped her forehead on her apron and smiled. "I really love this time year, don't you, Rankin?"

"Yes—yes, I really do, Mae."

Mae thought about A. G. and his friendship with the other children. "Rankin, I have been thinking about A. G. and his family. They are our neighbors, and we have never even met them. We are so wrapped up in our own lives that we haven't given them any thought."

"Are you thinking about maybe inviting them to dinner?" Rankin smiled, as they seemed to read each other's minds. They did not even know how many children were in the family. "Let's tell the boys to go now and invite them before they make other plans." Rankin was excited over the prospect of getting to know their nearest neighbors.

David and Angus saddled their mules and rode toward A. G.'s home. They had never visited before but knew they could find it. A. G.'s family had bought the Barnes' old property a year back and probably built a new house or fixed up the Barnes' old home. It wasn't far. As a matter of fact, they could have walked the mile or two in a few minutes but enjoyed riding the mules instead of plowing with them. They rode into the lane and climbed down from their mules. The old homestead had been repaired and given a new coat of paint. It was not much larger than the Torrey place but had a great many more trees in the yard. They were mostly oaks that had lined the path to the house for hundreds of years. The huge trees dwarfed the house at the end of the path.

Leading the mules along the path toward the house, they heard a voice from up above: "Who goes there?"

Looking up, David saw a little figure perched on one of the limbs about midway up the tree. It was a little boy no older than four or five. "How did you get up there?" David asked.

"I climbed, of course."

"Does your mama know you're out here, sittin' in this big ol' tree?" David was curious to know why such a small child was allowed such an adventurous opportunity.

A. G. had heard the talking and made his way toward the boys.

"He's all right. He's always climbing on something. He ain't afraid of nothing. David Michael, you better get down out of that tree before I tell Mama."

"Don't you worry he'll fall and break his neck?" Angus asked.

"No, he's been doing that since he was four. He can climb just about anything and can almost outrun me, even with his little short legs. Mama says he was real little when he was born, and now he spends most of his time trying to prove he's as good or better at anything than most of us whose bigger."

"Well, your name is David, too? We'll just have to call you Michael or David Michael."

David Michael was pleased with his new name and replied, "Let's call me Michael, 'cause David Michael is what my mama calls me when she gets mad with me."

The boys met Mrs. Kelly and liked her at once. A. G. had two sisters, Mary and Katherine, and one other brother besides David Michael. The brother's name was Warren. They were surprised to hear that A. G.'s father, William, was killed in the Battle at Big Black. A. G. said that he never mentioned it, because his mother thought that people would think that they needed charity. Nevertheless, the Torrey's invitation was accepted as one from neighbor to neighbor with the promise to repay the invitation.

Angus wanted to stay for a while longer just to see what Michael would climb next, but David told him that it was time to go home so they could report the number of guests. There would be six more for dinner.

"My stars and body!" Rankin said upon being told the new number for dinner. "Mae needs to kill at least two more chickens and get a slab of beef from the smokehouse."

"Well, Mama," said David, "this was your own idea."

"I know, Son, and it's perfectly all right."

The desserts were cooling on the kitchen tables, the ham was out of the oven, and the chicken was frying. The smoked beef had been sliced and arranged on one of Grandma's large platters. As Mae put the beef on the tray, she realized that they had not counted Grandma. She did not eat much anyway, and the only problem they may have would be if someone told her they had forgotten to include her in the family count.

The tablecloths were spread and weighted down with the plates and silverware. The food was placed on the table just as the neighbors arrived. Mrs. Kelly had brought three loaves of homemade bread and a pound of fresh-churned butter. They chatted as though they had known each other for years, and if the truth be known, they were distantly related.

"I truly do believe that country folk are much more friendly than city folk," Mrs. Kelly remarked and asked that she be called Mary. The boys finished up their dessert and decided to go for a little walk in the woods. As they passed by the apple orchard, David saw a familiar sight perched up in one of the trees. "Come on down, Michael, and go with us on an adventure," he said. Michael scurried down from the tree and took David's hand. They walked to a clearing on the edge of a small grove of trees and looked out across a valley. The view of the mountains in the distance was breathtaking, and the new growth of green on the trees painted the sky.

The boys sat on top of the hill to take it all in. "Bet if I took a runnin' start and jumped as far as I could, I'd hit the other side of this valley." Michael's imagination was in high gear.

"Well, little Michael, why would you want to do that when you could just roll down this big old hill without breakin' your neck?" Richard was concerned about Michael's ambitious ideas.

It must be a wonderful feeling, Angus thought, *to be able to soar in the air above the beautiful landscape below, feel the breeze blow your hair, and feel the warm sun on your face.* In his mind's eye, he could see Michael doing that very thing. There was something about him that caused Angus to believe that Michael would accomplish great things.

The sun was beginning to set, and the boys started back. The sunset would have been beautiful, but they did not want to be caught in the woods after dark. On the way home, Angus vowed to himself that he would spend more time with little Michael. Warren and his little brother David Michael were great additions to their group, and the sisters were very nice. *Downright pretty,* George and Richard thought. They were at the age that boys really began to notice girls but didn't want the other guys to know they cared one way or another.

Mary and Catherine seemed interested in the boys but were not bold enough to start any conversations with them. The time for that would come later—much later. When the boys got home, the ladies had cleared the table, and the white tablecloths were already soaking in the big wash pot in the backyard. They had been scrubbed with some of the lye soap that Rankin and Mae had made and would be boiled when the morning wash was done.

Mary Kelly gathered her little brood, and they started toward home and the old Barnes homestead. "It makes me so sad to see those children without a father," Rankin said. "That little one needs a father's care."

"You know, Rankin, I think they will be all right. The boys are devoted to Mary, and I'm sure they can handle the work. We'll have the boys check from time to time to see if they can use help. We have to be discreet about it, though. We sure know how she feels about charity."

"I felt as though I'd known her for years, Mae. Did you learn anything about her family?" Mae was one of those people who could ask questions without being too obvious about motive.

"Mary's family came from somewhere north of here, and her maiden name is Wright. Mary Ruth Wright."

"I don't know any Wrights, so I guess she is not related to the Johnsons or the Torreys. If she was, I'm sure that Grandma would have mentioned it."

The spring moved on into harvest time, and the Torreys and the Kellys were becoming fast friends. A. G. and Angus worked side by side, switching farms from day to day. George and Richard spent as much time as possible with Mary and Catherine and were pleased to hear that Grandma had not pronounced them relatives of the Torreys.

The harvest began in earnest with the women canning the garden vegetables for the upcoming winter. In Arkansas, it could get very cold, and between the field work and the garden picking, wood had to be chopped for the two families. The boys, who were in charge of the wood chopping, thought it an excellent idea for the two families to move into one house, and they would only have to chop enough wood to get one of the houses heated for the winter. Rankin and Mae would only laugh as they tried to imagine the chaos of a house with five boys and two girls trying to get along together.

The normal day would usually end with A. G. and Angus in the woods, tracking animals, or by the creek, fishing for the big one; George and Richard at the Kelly house, visiting with Mary and Catherine; Sarah and Alexandra playing together under the big walnut tree outside; David, William, and Warren playing mumbly peg; and David Michael sitting in the top of an apple tree at the Torreys', looking at the mountains in the distance.

Someday I'll climb that mountain, he thought.

Chapter 10

It was 1870, and Elizabeth had been away at college for a time in Clinton, Mississippi. Mississippi College was owned by the Presbyterian church at one time but was transferred to the control of the Baptists in 1842. During this time, Elizabeth lived with one of Papa's great-aunts, Lucy Johnson, in her home next to China Hill. China Hill was a beautiful, large Antebellum home that was built in 1840 on the streets of Clinton. During the Civil War, General Blair camped on the lawn of this home while preparing for the battle at Vicksburg. Just down the street from China Hill was another fine Antebellum home with purple violets growing on all the banks surrounding the house. It was also built in 1840 and called Violet Banks.

Aunt Lucy's home was not nearly as grand as these but was comfortable and within walking distance of the school. Most of the business area had been burned by the Yankees, but at the persuasion of a prominent Clinton resident, with connections up North, Mississippi College and Hillman College were spared. Most of the fine homes were burned to the ground and served as a reminder to Elizabeth of the South's great sacrifices and ultimate defeat.

Elizabeth met some of the boys who had been in a regiment called the Mississippi Rifles. They had been members of the Eighteenth Mississippi Regiment and fought in the very first battle of Manassas. Some had even witnessed General Lee's surrender at Appomattox.

Elizabeth saw the tattered company flag they had returned home to Clinton. This flag and the town were as close as Elizabeth came to the real destruction the war brought. It left her with an empty feeling inside. Now Elizabeth was home from college with more questions than answers. Seated in the parlor, Elizabeth and Anna, as in earlier times, waited for Papa's wisdom.

"Papa," Elizabeth began, "I can't get my head wrapped around all the problems we are having in our world today. I don't understand why God allows all the killing and cruelty that's going on. The slaves are freed and go up North where nobody seems willing to help them. They have no jobs and are hungry and freezing. The carpetbaggers come down South to get rich on our misfortunes by buying up our farms for less than half what they are worth. Papa, I heard at college that in the war, over one million men were killed or wounded. I feel like we are still living on the other side of the flood. What's to become of us?"

Anna began to cry, touched by her sister's compassion and concern. Papa looked at his girls and thought, *How have they grown up so fast?* "God has a way of dealing with every situation—a divine plan for us—but this world we live in with its problems is not God's doing, He only allows it. Since Adam and Eve, we have made wrong choices, and sin has made us the creatures we are now. Sometimes we get overwhelmed with our situation and forget who is in control. You know, as Christians, we are to obey God's law and follow the example of Jesus."

Elizabeth looked into her father's face. "Papa, I know that we must leave things in God's hand, and I can't do anything by myself, but maybe there is a job that He has for me to do."

"Pray about it, Elizabeth."

It was time for Elizabeth to return to school for her last year. Papa took her back to Aunt Lucy's house in the buggy. Mama packed a nice lunch with enough for Papa to have a bite on his long return home. It would be an all-day drive to Aunt Lucy's and then back home. Mama sent some of her canned vegetables and a very precious smoked ham to

Aunt Lucy. Most of their hogs had to be sold to help cover the expense of seed and for items they could not grow on the farm.

When the buggy arrived in Clinton, Papa turned down the muddy street in front of Mississippi College. The burned-out areas that were once places of business were depressing to see, and George got a sense of his daughter's depression. Not far down the street, the buggy rolled past China Hill, which still stood tall and proud, and on past Violet Banks, where the violets still grew. There were a few bullet holes on the south side of the building, but you would not notice them unless you looked very closely.

Down the street, Papa pulled the horse to a stop in front of Aunt Lucy's house. She could not imagine why her house had been spared unless it had something to do with the Johnson name. Aunt Lucy admitted that she was sure it had nothing to do with her good looks or "consortin' with the enemy."

Elizabeth took out Mama's basket of ham and canned goods for Aunt Lucy. They were well received, and Papa was invited to stay for tea and shortbread cookies baked by Aunt Lucy. Being polite, as Papa always was, he accepted and sat down in a big horse hair chair. The tea was nice and hot and the shortbread a treat, but the day was wearing on, and he wanted to get back to Tehvah by dark.

"Thank you, Aunt Lucy, for the tea and shortbread. Nobody makes shortbread like you do."

"Scones, George. They're scones," she corrected him.

"Oh, yes—scones, Aunt Lucy. I had forgotten what an amazing cook you are."

"George Torrey, you old flatterer. I love you anyway."

That was about as close to lying as Elizabeth had ever heard her father come. She tucked her chin and smiled a knowing grin. Papa saw the grin, and understanding its meaning, gave her a little wink. He told Aunt Lucy good-bye, and Elizabeth walked with him to the buggy. "Be careful on the way home, Papa. I hear that sometimes there are wandering bands of fierce Choctaw Indians on the trails." She smiled. Papa cocked his head to one side and looked at her over a crooked smile.

On the way home, George opened the little basket Flora had packed for them. Taking a fried chicken drumstick out of a napkin, he felt compelled to thank God for such a thoughtful wife. He chuckled to himself as he thought of praying that she had also included a fried apple pie somewhere in the mix.

It was late when George arrived home. He thought that he would write Elizabeth a nice long letter and tell her about the roving band of Choctaws who closed in on him and captured his chicken leg.

The horse came to a stop in front of Tehvah, and to George's relief, Zeb came out to meet him. "Let me take your hoss and buggy, Mr. George. I feed the hoss and water 'im for you."

"Thank you, Zeb; you're a good friend. I am quite tired after that trip. I must be getting old." George and Zeb had become fast friends, grateful to each other for entirely different reasons, and yet the same.

"How is Simmy feeling today, Zeb?"

"She fine, 'cept for bein' sick in the mornin'. Miss Flora say most folk havin' li'l babies gets that way at first." Simmy was in her third month, and for someone who had not wanted any children, she was very happy.

George went inside and was at once attacked by Anna. "You make your old papa feel so welcomed. You are always so happy to see me."

"That's because I love you so much, Papa."

George could hardly believe that Anna was fifteen years old. He did not like to think about Anna growing up and getting married, but at the same time, he knew that the time was near. He had thought of letting her take a trip to Arkansas to meet her cousins. There were not too many young folks her age in the little community, and she really did not know how to interact with her own age group. He felt that she was very far advanced for her age; yet she was still just a child in his mind.

"Miss Anna, did I ever tell you how much fun my cousins and I had playing together when we were your age?"

"Once in a while, you told me about hunting deer and turkey with them and sometimes about that old rope swing over the creek."

George realized that he had done quite a bit of reminiscing with the girls about his childhood and his beloved cousins. "I wish you could get to know your cousins the way I knew mine—you know, so you would have someone to share secrets with and have fun with."

"Oh, Papa, I've got you and Mama, Elizabeth and Simmy."

"Anna, Elizabeth is away at college, and when she finishes, she will more than likely get married or go away from home to teach school. Your mama and I will always be here to talk to when you need us. Simmy is going to have a little baby soon, and that baby will take up most of her time. I want you to have people your own age for friends."

"Papa, are you trying to get rid of me?" she asked with a smile.

"Anna, you know that's not true. Don't even tease about that. You will always be my little princess. I just thought you and I might take a little train trip up to Arkansas where we could visit our cousins at the same time."

"Now that would really be a treat, Papa. I think I would love to take a trip like that!"

George smiled, gave a little sigh of relief, and thought the idea of including himself in the trip was truly inspired. "Well, when the planting is done, I'll write my cousins John and Neill to see what they have to say. I would never invite myself to someone's house unless they were closely related enough to say no to the visit if the time was not right. You know, Cousin Neill has a daughter the same age as you. Her name is Sarah Catherine. My other cousin, John, has a daughter fourteen years old, and her name is Alexandra Mae."

"Do they have any boys, Papa?"

"Well, yes, there are five boys all together, and their names are Angus, Will, George, John, and Richard."

"Oh my, Papa; that's a lot of boys. Do you think that they will like me well enough to let me go places with them?"

Something told Papa that his sweet Anna was trying to make him jealous. This little tactic seemed to be inborn and was well-known by George. He couldn't believe the discomfort he felt and tried in vain not to let it show, but it was too late.

"Oh, Papa, you will always be my favorite beau." She smiled a coy smile that George didn't even know she had. It was just a natural thing for her to do. She turned and left the parlor. Anna had accomplished all she had intended to do. George scratched his head. *What was that? Maybe this visit is long overdue, or maybe we should just head for a monastery.* George sat down to collect his thoughts before composing his letter to his cousins in Arkansas.

Elizabeth seemed content with going to Mississippi College and pursuing her education. Ever since Elizabeth could remember, she had wanted to be a teacher. There had been no mention of boys except for the brief conversation about the Mississippi College Rifles. She had been quite impressed with their bravery—although not quite so excited about the killing of other men. George always thought that Elizabeth would be more concerned with tackling some great cause than becoming a wife and mother. This was fine with George, although at some point in time, he wanted a grandchild or two. Now he believed that Anna might be the best vehicle for the fulfillment of this particular dream. George at last sat down at his big roll-top desk and picked up his pen and paper. This time, he would address the letter to John and Neill; no need to offend anyone by leaving them out. He loved both of his cousins the same in spite of his strong resemblance to Neill. He dipped the pen into the ink and began to write, "Dear John and Neill ..."

Chapter 11

In Arkansas, the planting had begun, and most days, the boys spent their time hard at work in the fields. The garden planting was left mostly to the girls, and at times, Mrs. Kelly lent a hand in the garden or with the quilting. The fruits of their labors were always shared, and the Kellys did not view this as charity, because they worked hard alongside their friends. Now when Michael climbed up the trees, it was to pick fruit. There were still plenty of dried apples for Rankin's famous apple pies. The quilting went much faster in Arkansas than it did in Mississippi because of their sheer numbers. Mrs. Kelly, Rankin, Mae, Sarah, and Alexandra all were busy stitching; they had twice the beds to cover. March and April were busy times on the farm. The planting had to be done, quilting still went on, and the jars from the past year's canning had to be thoroughly cleaned. There were still everyday chores, such as milking, churning, feeding animals, and egg-gathering.

The boys went into the woods in search of bee hives, where they—with some degree of pain—gathered honey combs. The girls knew how to determine the good mushrooms from the poisonous ones, and they were good cooked on the stove in fresh butter and cream.

The family made lye soap and candles once a year. It was all hard work, but with help, it didn't seem to take long to accomplish. They felt blessed to have so much in the two large and happy families.

There was still a slight chill in the air, but everyone could tell that warmer weather was on the way. Neill had just come home from town, where he purchased the things they needed that could not be raised on the farm. He exchanged canned goods, dried apples, eggs, and milk for these goods. He got sugar, flour, coffee, and meal. The smokehouse provided all the meat they could use. As he pulled the wagon on to the grounds, he tied the horse and ran across the yard. "John," he shouted, "we got another letter from George." Neill was excited, especially when he saw his name in first position on the envelope.

"Open it, Neill. What's he got to say? I sure hope that it isn't bad news." Neill walked to the front porch of John's house, sat down on the steps, and fumbled with the envelope. He and John truly loved their cousin, and it was a treat to get any word from him. He had been there for them the year they had no seed to plant a decent crop to see them through the winter and the year they had so much family sickness.

Neill opened the letter and began to read.

Dear John and Neill,

I hope that this letter finds you and yours well. It has been difficult here since we lost our little Hugh; yet I know that he is with the Lord and has Mama and Papa to play with him. I don't know what I would do without that blessed assurance. I hope that you will never know the sorrow of losing a child.

How is the hunting in Arkansas this season? Have either of you been able to kill anything of worth? How I would love to go hunting with you boys and show you how it's done once again.

I guess the boys are just about grown. I hope they have at least half the fun together that we had when we were growing up.

Are you planting cotton again this year or rice? It gets harder to make any money on cotton, but with the help of the field hands, we manage. We still have our garden, and our smokehouse is well stocked. Some Arkansas apples would be mighty tasty. I remember what fine pies Rankin and Mae used to make.

Yesterday I was talking with my youngest daughter about doing some traveling on the train. Now I know it isn't polite to invite yourself someplace, but since it is you boys, I just might make an exception.

I was wondering about the possibility of Anna and me paying you a short visit. She's a sweet little girl, and as you know, the same age as Sarah—and as you already know, I am a fine, upstanding gentleman. You don't have to agree to that last remark, but I really would like for Anna to get to know her cousins and appreciate her family like we do. If this seems agreeable to you, write and let me know so that we can set up a time that would be agreeable for you and your family. I promise you that we won't stay longer than a year. The planting would all have to be done, and the garden as well, but we can work all that out later. If you feel that you just can't stand a visit from your champion hunter cousin from Mississippi, just let me know.

Your cousin,

George Edward Torrey

John and Neill looked at each other for a moment. "I can't believe it, Neill. That will be just about the best present in the world to have ol' George and his little one with us."

"Well, we need to write him right back. I hate to think we didn't invite him the last time we wrote him, but who would have thought George would leave his big old Tehvah to come and stay in our little old house in the Arkansas hills?"

"I don't know," John continued, looking out at the green hills that ran along the side of their land. "I don't think I would trade all this even for that fine house sittin' on all that land."

"Well, I'm glad he wasn't too shy to bring it up himself." Neill grinned, showing perfect white teeth. "He never was known to be too shy."

"Yes," laughed John, "the important thing is that he wants to come. He really wants to come and stay with us for a while."

"John, first we need to talk with Rankin and Mae about it and when they think a good time for the visit would be. I think they will be happy about the visit, but you know they will have to fuss with getting things ready."

Neill was always very considerate of his wife, Rankin. This was something that his mother had taught him because of all the benefits it brought. The fact that Rankin was such a beautiful woman did not hurt. She was tiny—no more than five feet tall with clear blue eyes and dark hair. Her sister-in-law was just the opposite—tall, dark brown eyes, and black hair. Mae's pride was her long black hair, while Rankin prided herself on her tiny, eighteen-inch waist.

John and Neill decided that each would go home and make the announcement to his family. The houses were built side-by-side, but the most important part of the arrangement was that the two women got along. They had always been friends and had very few disagreeable moments. They did their canning and quilting together and enjoyed each other's company.

The news of the visit was exciting for Mae and Rankin. They began to make plans for the visit immediately. "They aren't coming today," called John over the excited chatter of the two women.

"Never too early for planning," Mae answered over her shoulder. "I think it would be best for them to decide on when they want to visit." Mae was usually first to get the plans started. She had always been good with organizing, and Rankin didn't mind. She was content to follow along and help by doing what Mae suggested. Mae's eyes would sparkle with excitement as she unfolded her ideas to Rankin. There was no disharmony between them.

"We need to decide on the sleeping arrangements, Mae. What do you think?"

"I was thinking, Rankin, since you have five children, it might be best if Anna stayed with you and bunked with your Sarah. My boys can sleep anyplace. That would give George a room to himself."

Richard stuck his head into the room with a puzzled expression on his face. "Daddy just read me Cousin George's letter about their visit. I'm glad they are coming, but are they really going to stay for a year?"

Rankin laughed. "No, Son, Cousin George was just joking about that."

"Well, I'm kinda glad, because I'd hate to sleep on a pallet for a whole year!"

The next morning, everyone was still excited about the news of the visit. David finished his breakfast and headed to the field. As he passed the henhouse, he noticed feathers on the ground. Upon further investigation, he discovered that two of the laying hens were gone. He ran back to the house to get Neill.

"Looks like we had a fox in our henhouse." Neill was concerned. "Seems like we just can't enjoy anything without some kind of problem coming up." Neill was upset about losing his good laying hens. "John," he called to his brother. "Better get out here and talk about our bandit."

John came out of the house. "What's the matter, Neill?"

Neill looked concerned. "I guess it was a fox, John. He got two of the laying hens."

"I guess we are in for some more all-night vigils," said Neill. "You know that he'll be back, and we've got to get him."

"You know who'd love this all-nighter?"

"Yeah," answered Neill, a big grin on his face. "Ol' George."

The boys were excited about the possibility of shooting a big fox right in the henhouse. They decided to take turns and each have a shift.

"Boys, I know you are capable of putting this fox down, but it's not the same as out in the woods," John began. "I'm a little concerned that you might shoot something besides the fox."

"Like what, Uncle John?" asked George.

"Like each other," answered his uncle with a slight grin on his face.

"I'm cut to the quick, Uncle John."

"Well, that's better than being shot." They all laughed but realized that losing laying hens was no laughing matter. John and Neill went inside and loaded up their shotguns so that they could make the largest pattern of shot possible in order to rid themselves of this unwelcome varmint.

"I guess the best way to handle this would be to take shifts," said John.

Neill placed his loaded shotgun back on the rack inside the house. "Just tell me what shift you want me to take," he answered

After supper that same night, John and Neill picked up their guns and started out. They decided to both go instead of pulling two shifts. This would also insure that neither one would fall asleep. They sat on the ground with their backs against the side of John's house. The moon was full, and the wind blew slightly through the leaves of the apple trees, casting playful shadows on the ground. It would be hard to distinguish between the dancing shadows and the movement of any varmints creeping around in the moon light. Guns across their laps and pointed in opposite directions, they sat as still as possible and held their soft whispers to a minimum.

"No problem seeing that ol' fox tonight," whispered Neill. "And he won't have much trouble seeing us even in the shadow of your house."

As the night wore on—long past John's normal bedtime—his eyes began to get very heavy.

Neill sat forward slightly. "Listen. I heard something over there in the edge of the woods." He looked at John and pointed in the direction of the noise he heard. They sat motionless and waited. A dark figure cautiously emerged from the woods into the bright light of the moon. It was a raccoon.

Neill, a bit disappointed, lowered his gun. "Well, that's a bandit all right, but I don't think he's a chicken thief."

"No, he's probably after eggs, but the roosters will make short work of his raid."

John slapped his hand on the ground beside him, and the coon made a hasty retreat into the safety of the darkened woods.

Hours passed. "It must be twelve o'clock," John said with a yawn.

"You never could stay up past nine o'clock, John. Just go on in and go to bed before you fall asleep and shoot me!"

There was another rustling in the woods, and a figure built much lower to the ground crept toward the chicken house.

"Well, can you see him, Neill?"

"Of course I see him. Looks like a red fox to me. He's big and looking to get bigger on our chickens."

"Let me take a look." John was excited and took a peek around Neill's shoulder.

"You gonna shoot him, Neill?"

"Do you want to shoot him, John?"

"Oh, for goodness sake, let's both shoot him. Neill, you take the end with the white tip, and I'll get the end that's headed for the hen house."

"Why do I get the tail?"

"Just shoot before he has a chance to put the hens in a bag."

Boom! Both guns fired at the same instant, and fur flew in all directions. "He never knew what hit him," Neill said, quite pleased that they had rid the farm of a chicken-eating varmint. In a matter of minutes, boys were steaming out of both houses, pulling on their pants over long underwear.

"Did you get him? Sounded like all-out war out here. Where is he?" George was most interested to see the evidence. His father sometimes liked to elaborate on the truth.

"He's distributed all along the woods nearest to the hen house," John said with a grin on his face.

"You missed him, didn't you?" Richard knew how John and Neill could skirt the truth with some ridiculous tale. The boys immediately ran to the edge of the woods to see if there was any truth to the tale.

"*Ugh!*" David made a face at the sight. "Looks like you ran him through the cotton gin."

The night was ending, and John and Neill retired for a few hours' rest before the day's work began. The boys were all wide awake and in Neill's house, talking about the big fox murder. They were anxious to see the evidence in the broad daylight.

"I call the tail," said Angus, who had visions of a cap similar to the famous Davy Crockett's coonskin variety.

"If the tail met the same fate as the rest of that fox, you'll have to sew it together in fifteen pieces," David said with a laugh. "I didn't know a fox could be divided into so many little pieces."

The boys sprawled out for a quick nap before the sun came up. They were awakened by the bustling in the kitchen, where the breakfast dishes were being cleared. They had slept through breakfast.

Grabbing biscuits, the boys rushed outside to see the gruesome sight in the light of day. They ran to the edge of the woods to find no sign of the massacre from that night. They looked at each other with wonder on their faces. Had they all dreamed the very same dream?

Angus saw his sister, Alexandra, and his cousin, Sarah, playing near one of the apple trees in the orchard. Not wishing them to have any unpleasant dreams about the carnage, he asked, "Have you two seen any animals around here or any fox tails?"

"We did," Sarah answered without looking up from her play.

"Well, where did you see it?"

Alexandra looked up at her brother with a sad smile. "It was over there by the woods. Would you like to see where we buried him?"

Chapter 12

The letter from Arkansas came to Mississippi at last, but not the one George was looking for. Grandma Torrey, John and Neill's mother, was ill, and the doctor did not hold out much hope for the ninety-year-old lady. John and Neill thought it prudent for George's family to come as soon as possible if they wanted to see Grandma Torrey before she left this world.

George, Flora, and Anna packed their things, and Zeb drove them to the depot.

John met the family at the depot in Arkansas with the buggy and drove them to his home.

"Wish this could be under better conditions," John said with a sigh. "I don't think that Mama really wants to stay."

"Sounds just like our Izzy before she died," George replied. "She let us know in no uncertain terms that she was ready to go, and we needed to just let her leave."

"It's really hard," John continued. "Sometimes she thinks she's in Scotland with Papa, and she makes it sound so real, you'd swear you were on the Firth of Clyde."

The wagon rolled up in front of the house, and all the children came out to meet their kinfolk.

Neill came out on the porch, and Anna gasped a little. She couldn't believe how much he looked like her own papa. She decided that she liked him right away.

A. G. had come for the arrival and could not take his eyes off Anna. He thought she was just about the prettiest girl he had ever seen.

Anna, Sarah, and Alexandra went inside just as though they had known each other for years. They went into Grandma's room to tell her hello before going into Sarah's room, where the three girls were to stay. Grandma hugged Anna and told them to be sure to speak to Grandpa, too.

George and Flora came into the room to greet Aunt Sarah. "Oh, George," she said, "how good to see you. You came just when I knew you would. Did you see all the heather on the hills?"

"Yes, Aunt Sarah, I can close my eyes and see that purple carpet." He had heard it described by his own mother and father so many times, he actually thought he could visualize it.

"Even though there's still snow in the mountaintops, you can see those beautiful yellow craig bushes, and there are green pastures behind those stone walls. There are lots of sheep this year, even more than last."

"Isn't Scotland beautiful this time of the year, Aunt Sarah?" George's voice trailed off, and he turned his head away from Grandma. Even though she was his aunt, he loved her like a mother. Flora spent some time with Aunt Sarah and was transported to a new land, and it was beautiful.

That night, they gathered at Neill's home for supper, and Neill asked George to return their thanks. He began, "Holy Father, giver of every good and perfect gift, creator and sustainer of our very beings, we praise your holy name. We know that your servant is ready to enter your kingdom, and we pray that you will allow us to let her go in peace. Help her to know how very much we all love her, and pray for her comfort. We pray you would send your holy angels to lead her home. Bless us all now in this time together, and for the blessings we are about to receive, make us truly thankful. In Jesus' name. Amen."

That night, Grandma slipped away quietly, and in the morning light, she looked as though she was sleeping.

The funeral service at the small community church was more a celebration of Grandma Torrey's life. Adults she had taught in Sunday school when they were very small, people she had helped nurse back to health from illness, and people with whom she had prayed in years past were there to show their respect. She was buried in the small churchyard cemetery beside Grandpa. A tall obelisk marked the graves.

One side read, "George McNeill Torrey, Beloved husband and father. Born 5-9-1773. Died 3-9-1852." Already carved on the other side were the words, "Sarah Elizabeth Buie Torrey, Beloved wife and mother. Born 11-4-1780. Died."

The cousins made the return trip home in the flat bed wagon, boys in the back and men up front. The ladies were driven home in the buggies of some community church members from Scotland Presbyterian Church. How appropriate that Grandma and Grandpa were sleeping in Scotland.

"Sure a lot of sweet things to remember about that lady. She didn't leave us empty," George said, thinking of other times.

"Yes," said Neill with a smile, "but you never had to learn the catechism from Mama. If you had enough time to study a question and couldn't give the answer, she would threaten you with a peach tree limb."

John chuckled. "Well, we learned it, didn't we?" The conversation went to the lighter side, and they shared stories about Grandma Torrey and her quick wit.

"I don't think Aunt Sarah would want us to be sad. I'm sure that she would tell us just to be glad she got there." George was trying to get in on all the uplifting talk of his aunt's wit but was not as adept as his cousins. They had always been able to turn a situation to the lighter side without any effort.

A. G. had ridden home with the boys. He had become quite attached to Grandma Torrey since he went home with the boys on that first day and wanted to honor her memory by attending her funeral.

The ladies had already arrived home and were at Neill and Rankin's house, setting the table with the food that came from the ladies at the church and the bread baked by Mary Kelly. The smell of the bread made A. G. hungry, but that hunger for food soon left him. Anna walked out the door, and she had his full attention. *When she goes back to Mississippi tomorrow, I'll probably never see her again,* he thought. Since he believed this to be the case, he walked toward the porch where she was seated. He could hardly believe his newfound courage.

Anna looked up to see who was walking toward her. Her dark brown eyes seemed to be smiling, and her black curls hung from both sides of the blue and white bonnet that was tied neatly under her chin. His heart thumped wildly as he looked at the little rosebud lips that smiled at him. He felt that he might lose the biscuits that he had for breakfast. Yes, he was older than Anna, but of one thing he was certain—he was in love with Miss Anna Torrey of Tehvah in the state of Mississippi.

"Hello, A. G. It was so nice of you to come to our aunt's funeral."

A. G. smiled at Anna. "I wouldn't have missed it—I mean, I couldn't have stayed away." *Oh, I'm such an idiot; I don't even know what to say to her.* "I wish you could stay a while longer. There are lots of things to see around here." *Like what? The pig pen, the chicken house?* He would have to come up with more than that. He would give some thought to what made this place so very special to him.

Anna looked up at A. G. and smiled. "We are planning on a return trip."

A. G. could hardly contain his excitement. "When—when do you think you'll be coming back?"

"Whenever Papa decides," Anna said with a smile as she at last realized that A. G. was smitten.

A. G. grew a bit bolder and seated himself beside Anna to resume their conversation. He hoped that Anna could not hear the pounding of his heart when a voice rang out from a nearby apple tree. "Anna and A. G., sittin' in a tree ..." It was his pesky little brother.

"David Michael, get out of that tree, and go home or go inside. They got apple cake in there, and I hear it's going fast." Michael jumped quickly to the ground, and A. G. felt that a catastrophe had been avoided.

Inside Neill's house, the cousins had settled in with all the stories of their youth. Most were funny, but some were filled with what they called bravery.

"How about the time at the creek when we were swingin' out over the water on that old rope swing?" George's eyes widened as he told the story. "Remember? That old rope broke just as I took off, and I landed on my head, knocked out colder than a hammer. I was laid out over that old log in the pond like a fish to be cleaned."

"Yes," Neill replied, "and I had to go in and bring you back to the bank."

"Oh, brave, big boy," was John's reply. "The only reason you did was because Mama had made apple pie for supper, and you were afraid that it'd all be gone if we waited for old George to wake up."

"Well, my brother John wouldn't go in to get you, because he didn't want to get his pants wet."

At an earlier point in time, this would have caused a major scuffle, but now there was only hearty laughter. *Maybe we are a bit too flippant at this time.* George felt a bit guilty about the laughter right after Aunt Sarah's funeral.

Neill raised his head and looked at George. "You know how Mama was—nothing would please her more than to know we were enjoying ourselves with old stories about our childhood. She loved that sort of thing."

"Well," George said, "I sure do remember how she laughed at the knot on my head after she knew that I didn't have a concussion."

"I don't know when we will be able to visit again with Elizabeth about to graduate from college. I really don't know what her plans are. She is so wrapped up in her own little world and all the things she considers to be wrong, we really don't talk much anymore. She used to value my opinion, but you know how she thinks she has the answer to all the world's problems. It really is true that a little knowledge is a dangerous thing."

John ventured his opinion on Elizabeth. "She seems to have compassion for everything and everybody. I don't think that's such a bad thing. It's the way people—really serious people—get things done. Elizabeth might wind up in Washington."

George smiled. "I'd be happy just to see her washing some diapers."

Anna walked in from the porch, and Sarah and Alexandra grabbed her by the arms and guided her toward Sarah's room.

"Okay," Sarah whispered, "what's going on with you and A. G.?"

"Why, whatever do you mean?" she asked in her most mocking Southern drawl.

"Anna Jane Torrey." Alexandra looked a bit perplexed. "You know exactly what we mean!"

"Oh, dear. Do you mean that cute little ol' redheaded boy by the name of A. G.?"

"Who else you been talking with out there on the porch?" Sarah asked.

"And that's all it was. Talk. You two been spying on me? I can't believe it!" Anna tucked her chin so that her cousins would not see the sly little smile, but they both knew that it was there. "Besides, we are leaving in the morning for Mississippi, and I doubt Mrs. Kelly would let her son travel that far from home."

Alexandra looked at Sarah and whispered loudly, "Oh, he'll wait; won't he, Sarah?"

"Oh, yes; he'll wait. A. G.'s in love."

George and his family rose early the next morning along with all of John's family and all of Neill's family. Neill would drive them into town to the train station.

After their breakfast of scrambled eggs and thick-sliced bacon from the smokehouse, George had a second cup of coffee and began his good-byes and thanks for a very pleasant stay, except for Aunt Sarah's funeral. He promised John that they would make a return visit soon.

As Anna climbed into the buggy, she noticed that A. G. made the early morning trip to see her off. She smiled approvingly at him and looked in the direction of Sarah and Alexandra. Their hands were covering their mouths so the knowing giggles would not be heard. Anna shielded her mouth on both sides with her hands and poked her tongue out at her two cousins. This only made the giggles worse, and Anna had to laugh.

"Well, what was that all about?" George asked, rather puzzled by Anna's actions. "Just little girl stuff, I guess."

"I don't know whether or not you have noticed, George, but those little girls are growing up into young ladies."

"Neill, are you talking about Sarah?"

"Well, George, Anna and Sarah are the exact same age."

They arrived at the station and went inside to purchase tickets for the trip back home. George had sent a telegram to Tehvah with instructions as to time of arrival, asking if Zeb would be kind enough to meet the train at the depot.

The train was running a little late, and Papa sat down next to Anna on a little wooden bench just by the door. People had carved their names and initials into the bench while waiting for the train.

Papa looked at the carvings, "My goodness. Why would anyone do such a thing?" Anna shrugged her shoulders, not particularly interested in this line of conversation, and Papa went on with the subject of defacing public property. "Your grandma used to say that a fool's name, like a fool's face, is was always stuck in some public place. How do you feel about A. G. Kelly, Anna?"

The question threw Anna back into the reality of the moment. "Why would you ask such a question as that, Papa?"

"I just wanted to know for myself."

"Oh, Papa, are you jealous?"

"I suppose I am a bit jealous. You once told me that I would always be your beau."

"Well, Papa, at some point in time, you are just going to have to get over me—but not any time soon, I promise."

The sound of the train whistle could be heard from far down the track. Picking up two bags, George thought, *I hope that you can keep that promise, little lady.*

Zeb, ever dependable, was waiting for the family as the train rolled into the station. Zeb helped with the luggage, and they all climbed into the buggy.

"How are things at Tehvah, Zeb? I know we haven't been gone very long, but I wondered if you had enough help and also how Simmy was doing."

"Everything fine. Simmy gettin' fatter and fatter."

"I'd say she has a good reason, Zeb, wouldn't you? I hope you haven't told that to Simmy. You know, women don't like being told that they are getting fat or that they look fat."

"Oh, Simmy don't care, Mr. George; she proud of her fatness, 'cause it be a baby."

Two weeks after the family returned home from their visit, things seemed to be getting back to normal when a letter came from Arkansas. George thought that it was a newsy letter from his cousins, but to his surprise, it was addressed to "Miss ANNA Torrey."

"Well, how nice of Cousin Sarah to drop you a line," George said with a smile.

"Papa, it isn't from Sarah at all. It happens to be from A. G."

George winced. "I had no idea that he could even write. He never struck me as the studious kind."

Anna tore open the letter in great anticipation and began to read.

Dear Miss Anna,

    I hope that you don't mind me writing you this letter. I didn't get much time to talk with you when you and your family were here, and I wanted to know lots of things about you.

    I don't think your papa likes me too much, but I don't know why. I sure do admire him.

    What do you like to do? What's your favorite flower? What food do you like to eat? I just really want to know all about you.

    Please write back to me and tell me if your papa has decided when your next visit will be. I think about you most all the time.

Yours truly,

Angus G. Kelly

"What did the boy have to say, Anna?"

"Papa! That's for me to know. Oh, he did mention you. He said that he didn't think you liked him very much."

"I'm sorry that I gave that impression, but I will say that he is very perceptive." George walked down the hall to the west room, feeling a little ashamed of his reaction to the letter and his feelings in general about A. G. After all, what chance could a long-distance romance have? They were both young, and what was the old adage about "out of sight, out of mind"? Then George recalled another one about absence making the heart grow fonder. George was rethinking his return to the Arkansas hills. Those thoughts were soon replaced with those of Elizabeth's graduation from Mississippi College in Clinton.

The family would go to Clinton, spend the night with Aunt Lucy, and see their eldest daughter receive her diploma. She had mentioned staying in Clinton, where she would teach at a school dedicated to the education of young black children. This was a dream of Miss Sarah Dickey and was just the sort of thing that George thought Elizabeth would do. It was not a get-rich plan but a noble one.

Anna spent most of her waking hours waiting for the mail to arrive from Arkansas. She couldn't stand the fact that she would be gone for two whole days and might miss a letter when it actually arrived. Nevertheless, she packed her best Sunday dress in preparation for Elizabeth's graduation.

The following day, the family loaded the buggy with their bags and a lunch for the trip. The ride seemed longer than usual for George, but they arrived in time to visit for a while with Aunt Lucy and Elizabeth before bedtime.

The big day had finally arrived, and the whole family drove down the street to Mississippi College and went into the auditorium. Signs of the recent conflict were still evident outside, with musket balls and grapeshot embedded in the walls of the chapel, but this did not detract from the joy of the moment.

Elizabeth wanted to explain her decision to stay and help Sarah Dickey at Mount Hermon Female Seminary, which was for the education of young black women. There were still plenty of black women in the area who needed educational opportunities. Clinton had two educational institutions that remained open during the Civil War. Mississippi College and Mount Hermon Female Institute were primarily for the education of young ladies who lived in nearby plantations and in the surrounding areas. It was very important to Miss Dickey that black women have the same opportunity, and Elizabeth had made that dream her own.

Elizabeth was touched by Sarah Dickey's life story of her mother dying when Sarah was only eight years of age. Her father, who had seven other children and no means of caring for all them, felt it necessary to give the children to other relatives. Education was a struggle for her.

When she was sixteen, she could not write but decided that she would learn. "What a life that lady led," Elizabeth said as she looked up dreamily. "I wish I could do something like that with my life."

George knew at that point that he would have to look elsewhere for any grandchildren. Elizabeth had set her sights on a life of sacrifice— and more than likely, poverty. George knew that this was her dream, and he had always tried to teach his daughters to follow their dreams. He was very proud of Elizabeth. She was totally unselfish and seemed to have found some meaning to her life.

Oh, Anna, George thought, *why can't you find a cause other than A. G. Kelly? George was having second thoughts about his little princess marrying ANYONE.*

Mama

Papa

Chapter 13

Elizabeth had begun her teaching duties at Mount Hermon Female Institute and was giddy with excitement. She was teaching literature and had ten students in her class. The girls ranged in age from thirteen to fifteen, and all seemed to be attentive and eager to learn.

"Good morning, class. My name is Elizabeth Torrey, and I was raised right here in Mississippi, just like you. I have one sister who lives at home with my mother and father in a little community called Scotland. I would like to know more about each one of you, so now I will call the roll, and when you hear your name, please answer 'present' and tell us anything you would like to tell about yourself and your family. Rosie Brown."

"Present." The voice was timid and soft. "I was born on a plantation not far from this school. My pappy left to go up north just after the war, and we ain't seen hide nor hair of him since." She sat down and breathed a sigh of relief. Elizabeth's heart ached for the tiny girl who was fourteen years old but very small for her age. Elizabeth was worried that she may have asked for more information than she needed.

"Sunshine Leeds."

Sunshine stood up and twisted side to side, fingers entwined and hands clasped in front of her. She flashed Elizabeth a big smile, and Elizabeth knew that she would remember this name and face.

"Present," she said with a smile. "My name Sunshine. That be a funny name for some folk, but my mama say it fit me fine, 'cause I be her ray of sunshine."

Elizabeth saw right away that they needed to work on the verb *be*.

"Ruthie Jackson." Elizabeth continued with the roll call.

A tall, thin girl of about fifteen stood. "I be Ruthie Jackson, and I comes from the same plantation as Rosie." The voice was that of hardness and discontent. "Born and raised a slave. That's what we is and apt to stay." She sat down with a thud.

"Tiny Bell Jones."

"I present and glad to be in your class, Miss Lizabeth. Let's see; I don't know how to start. My mammy and pappy fine, and I got me five brothers and a li'l sister. They worrisome sometime, but I still like 'em fine."

Elizabeth could see that she had a real talker, so she politely interrupted. "Thank you, Tiny Bell. I'm really glad to have you in my class and look forward to meeting your family." She continued. "Mary Henderson."

"Present." A beautiful young girl rose from her desk with a certain amount of dignity. She seemed confident yet reserved. Her skin was light and her eyes a beautiful shade of green. "My mother is always there to help me, but I don't know my father. I have no brothers or sisters, and I think I speak very good English."

"Indeed you do." Elizabeth was so impressed with Mary's demeanor and presence that she even had visions of Mary as her teacher's aide. "Precious Johnson."

A young girl of thirteen stood up. She was the exact opposite of Mary. She was short of stature and a little portly but smiled an impish grin that Elizabeth loved immediately. She looked like Anna with her muddy black face that day on the creek bank. Elizabeth felt an immediate connection to Precious.

"That's me, Miss Lizbeth. I present and 'counted for."

Oh my goodness, thought Elizabeth. *I can see I've got my work cut out for me as far as grammar goes.*

"I's from Dogwood plantation. I loves my mammy but ain't got no pappy; he runned off, and when they catched him, he got whooped within a inch of his life. He ain't been right since."

"Oh, Precious, I'm so sorry."

"You didn't do nothin', Miss Lizbeth!" Precious Johnson sat down and smiled up at Elizabeth.

The roll call continued through Sarah Ford, Lessie Speaks, and Mae Jones. "Thank all of you for sharing some of yourselves with me, because it helps me to know you better. We will be studying the subject of literature. Can anyone tell me what that involves?" Mary's hand shot into the air. "Yes, Mary?"

"That's like stories and poems and who wrote them."

"Very good, Mary." Elizabeth looked around the room for some sign of interest, and seeing none, continued. "I trust that we can all read a little bit. If not, there are people who will be happy to help you, I'm sure. I have a list of stories and poems that we will be studying and talking about in class. I will assign some that I believe you will enjoy."

Mary raised her hand once more. After Elizabeth acknowledged her, she asked her question. "Miss Torrey, could you give us an idea of what we will be asked to read?"

"Mary, since you seem to be so eager, I will give you the option to pick your own author and choose one of his works. They will include Washington Irvin, Longfellow, James F. Cooper, Walt Whitman, William Cullen Bryant, and Henry Thoreau. Some of these writers are a little deeper than others, and I will take that into consideration when I pass out the assignments. Mary, I would like to see you take a writer that would challenge you."

Mary nodded that she understood, and Elizabeth took that as a sign to continue   with her instruction. "I would like to see some of the younger girls read some of Longfellow's works, such as *Hiawatha* and *Evangeline* or Washington Irvin's *Rip Van Winkle* and *The Legend of Sleepy Hollow*. We will discuss with the class what we have read. I don't ask that you finish a work in one day but that you read slowly enough to enjoy and understand it."

After class, Mary came to Elizabeth's desk. "I thought that I might read *Leaves of Grass* by Thoreau or some work of Ralph Waldo Emerson, but I'm afraid that the other girls will feel that I think of myself as being too smart."

Elizabeth looked into Mary's beautiful green eyes and smiled. "Mary, you are smart, and I was hoping that you would take a work that would be a challenge. You know, it was Ralph Waldo Emerson who said, 'To be great is to be misunderstood.' I believe that you have the potential to be great, and I think that it would be such a help to me for you to be my assistant. The other girls do not have to know unless you would like for me to tell them, but I intend to rely heavily on your help with this class."

Mary smiled and embraced Elizabeth. "I think that I would be honored, Miss Torrey."

"Well, I know that I would be honored to have you."

The weeks went by rapidly, and Mary worked alongside Elizabeth, helping the younger children to read their own assignments as she continued with her own.

"You know, Miss Torrey, Henry Thoreau and Emerson were friends like we are, and they were both nonconformists."

Elizabeth smiled. "Like us, Mary?"

After a few months of one-on-one teaching by both Elizabeth and Mary, whom Elizabeth trusted completely, the children were reading, and their grammar had improved markedly. Elizabeth was pleased beyond words and wished that she could keep Mary with her, but she knew that would not be fair. Mary did not belong in Elizabeth's little class. She was ready for higher education and greater things. After the first school year ended, Elizabeth asked Mary to stay after the last class was finished.

Mary pulled a chair up to the front of Elizabeth's desk and sat down. "Am I being kept after school?"

Elizabeth laughed. "No, ma'am. I just have something that I would like to discuss with you. I don't think that I could have made the progress that was made this past school year without you; as a matter of fact, I know I couldn't have done it. I don't know how I will manage without you this next school year."

Mary's forehead wrinkled. "Am I being fired?"

"Of course not! I just don't think it's fair to you for me to hold on to you when you need to be moving on to higher education and better opportunities. Mary, I have written a letter to Mississippi College admissions and requested an interview for you. I want you to go on to Mississippi College, because you are ready. You are not to worry about tuition, because that is being worked out. You will be free to pursue an education in whatever field of study you wish, and you will be great!"

Mary's eyes widened, and then as reality set in, began to tear up. "I can't believe that you would do this for me!"

"I know many people who would do this for you. You are smart, eager to learn, and a genuine pleasure to be around. Everything about you simply reeks of success, and an attitude such as yours should be rewarded. One day, we will all be proud to say that we knew Mary Henderson. I don't want you to think that I'm trying to plan your future or telling you what you should do. That's for you to decide."

"There's no doubt in my mind that I would welcome this kind of an opportunity, and to think that you believe in me enough to set up this appointment is just too wonderful to imagine. Thank you so much. I won't let you down."

"That thought never even crossed my mind, I can assure you. I have you set up to talk with the Dean of Admissions on Tuesday morning at ten o'clock. He will help you get your forms filled out and give you further instructions. Is that a good time for you?"

Mary was overcome with excitement. "If you would go with me, it would be just about perfect."

"I can't think of any place that I'd rather be at that special time."

Tuesday morning came, and the two friends went in to see the Dean. All the necessary preliminary forms were completed, and arrangements were made for Mary to attend college. She was young to be starting college, but Elizabeth knew how very gifted she was. What could possibly go wrong with this decision to pursue a higher degree of learning?

On the following week, a representative arrived at the school where Elizabeth was working and informed her that due to Mary's age, they thought it best for her to wait a while longer before she embarked upon a college degree. This was heartbreaking news for Elizabeth, and she became determined to get Mary into a college-level program.

The next day, Elizabeth began to look into nearby colleges to contact on Mary's behalf. One way or another, Mary would go to college in the fall. This consumed Elizabeth's mind night and day; therefore, the telegram from Papa interrupted her thoughts, if only for a little while. The wire read, "Simmy is a mama! Little girl ... Anna Elizabeth ... calling her Izzy. Love, Papa."

How wonderful for Simmy and Zeb, she thought. *I guess before we know it, Anna will make an aunt out of this old maid schoolteacher.* She remembered the lesson she gave Anna on the birth of babies. *Well, maybe not.* She laughed to herself.

Chapter 14

At Tehvah, there was much bustling about. The cotton trade had begun to boom again, and George was shipping all the cotton his little plot of fields could produce. Zeb was excited, because he had a new little daughter and his own cotton field on which he grew cotton for a profit. It was still against the law in Mississippi to free a slave outright or for a slave to own any land. Because of this slight technicality, George and his field hands had a gentleman's agreement about the land they farmed, and each was very happy with the arrangement.

Simmy rocked her baby on the back porch of the main house while Zeb and George sat on the steps. "Zeb, I can't believe you and Simmy have a little girl." George smiled as he turned to look back at Izzy. "Wouldn't Izzy be proud of her namesake?"

"I recon she would, Mr. George." Simmy looked adoringly into the dark, chubby little face gazing back at her mother.

"If I remember correctly, someone decided a few years back that she didn't want any babies."

Simmy looked up at George. "Well, that was sure a crazy ol' gal what didn't know what she's talkin' 'bout."

"I know that's right," Zeb added.

"I been wishin' Miss Lizbeth could see her. You tell her 'bout my baby's name, Mr. George?"

"I sent her a telegram just last week. I'm sure that she'll be coming home to see Miss Izzy just as soon as she gets her class finished and finds a college that will allow her student to come and take a few college courses. I'm sure she is very honored to have you and Zeb name that baby for Anna and her."

"You thank Miss Lizbeth'll ever get married, Mr. George?"

"I don't know, Simmy. Right now, she seems to be married to her work. She really loves teaching those children."

"Surprise! Hello, where is everybody? I want to see that Anna Elizabeth, Izzy child." The familiar sound of Elizabeth's voice came down the hall with mama in tow. A screaming Anna ran down the stairs and embraced her sister.

"Oh, I've missed you," she said.

"Like old times," Elizabeth said as they skipped in celebration to the back porch. Elizabeth first gave Papa a bear hug and then shook hands with Zeb, who had a big grin on his face. In one swoop, she walked to Simmy's chair, kissed her on the forehead, and reached for the precious little brown bundle in Simmy's arms.

"Oh, you beautiful, wonderful little angel." Elizabeth held her securely as she stood looking into Izzy's little face, rocking her from side to side. "Simmy, I can hardly believe it. You have a precious little girl of your very own. I wish I could be here to play with her out in the backyard and just plain spoil her."

Anna was smiling. "Yeah, we could throw rocks at turtles in the creek."

"We are glad you decided to come for a little while, Elizabeth. I have a lot of questions to ask you about how your school year went."

"Why don't I fix us some sandwiches for supper?" Anna was already headed for the kitchen.

Elizabeth turned to look at her sister. "Can you manage that, Anna?"

"Why, Elizabeth, that's what I cook the best."

Little Izzy began to fuss, and Simmy knew that she must be hungry. Promising Elizabeth that she would bring her back shortly, Simmy took the baby from Elizabeth's arms and walked down the porch steps toward the Zebulon cottage.

Papa and Elizabeth moved down the hall and into the west room. "So tell me about this exceptional student that you are attempting to get into college." Papa had his own ideas about Elizabeth's dilemma but wanted to hear more facts from her on the subject.

"Well, Papa, I don't know exactly what happened. Mary is young, but she has such potential. She could teach my class as well as I and relate to the children even better than you could ever imagine."

George eyed Elizabeth thoughtfully. "I have been thinking about this since I heard your story. If the problem is money, our cotton crops have really been good—even better than before the war—and I can afford to contribute to this child's education."

"That is a wonderful idea, Papa, but money was never the real problem. I could possibly call on you at a later time to help me with letters of recommendation to some of the colleges close by that accept black children into their schools."

"That could indeed be one of the problems that you are facing."

"Hey, you two, come and get it. I have cooked up a batch of sandwiches for you." Anna approached to herd them into the kitchen to eat the bacon and tomato sandwiches that she had prepared for them. She had also set some cracklings on the counter in a little china bowl. "I remembered how much you like cracklings, Elizabeth."

"And do you also remember how sick they used to make me?"

"I recon I do, Miss Elizabeth. Now have a nice big serving."

"Some things never change." Elizabeth smiled as she sat down at the table in the kitchen.

After lunch, Elizabeth and Anna went upstairs to their room to talk while Papa read for a while. "I understand that you have developed quite an interest in the fine state of Arkansas, Anna," Elizabeth said, sitting down on her old bed. "You have anything you want to share with me about this lad?"

"Elizabeth, he's just the cutest thing. He's got big brown eyes and hair the color of a copper penny. He can hunt and fish and do just about anything he sets his mind on to do."

"My goodness, Anna; sounds like you've got yourself a real dream of a man—or you are really looking through the eyes of a girl in love."

"Papa told me that we would go back for another visit, but that hasn't happened yet. I've only visited two times—or three if you count Aunt Lucy's funeral. A. G. is three years older than I am, and I think that Papa has a problem with that, but look at Papa and Mama. You know that he is eight years older than Mama? Can you just imagine how Grandpa Gilchrist felt about that difference? Now here I am, seventeen years old, and he will soon be twenty. How long do you think he'll spend waiting for little ol' me?" The Southern drawl emerged once again from Anna, as it often did.

"Well, I'm twenty, and I thank the good Lord I have not as yet been bitten by that old love bug. Has he been to school, Anna, or has he set aside any money for the future?"

"He has been to school, but I don't know how much schooling he has had. I do know that he is not related to Cornelius Vanderbilt." Anna was beginning to be annoyed with Elizabeth's practical questions. All she wanted was to get approval and a little sympathy for her aching, lovesick heart.

"I'm sorry, Anna; it's just that I worry about you, and these things are important for anyone to consider who is looking for a new life with someone."

"His family has some land in Arkansas, but I never asked him how much or how profitable their cotton crop had been. Oh, Elizabeth, why do you have to be so practical? Why can't you just be happy for me?"

"I'm sorry, Anna. I am happy for you and A. G., and I promise you that I am really looking forward to meeting him."

"Elizabeth, you have to promise me that you won't ask him a lot of embarrassing questions."

"I promise, and when I get this college business off my mind, I'll ask Papa if you and I can pay our Arkansas cousins a little visit. If I can be the chaperone, I think Papa just might go for it."

"That would be wonderful, Elizabeth. Thank you so much." Anna gave her sister a hug, and they both went downstairs to look for Simmy and the baby.

"You remember when you gave me the birthing talk?"

"Let's never mention that again, please." Elizabeth knew that if she lived to be one hundred, she would never live that down.

The next morning, Elizabeth and Anna woke up early, but by the time they got dressed and went downstairs, Mama was already making coffee on the stove for Papa.

"It was so good to be able to talk with you yesterday face-to-face instead of by letter. I just know that you will be able to do something for Mary and her desire to go to college." Mama had waited until after Elizabeth's talk with Anna to have her talk time with her daughter. Flora had greeted Elizabeth when she arrived at Tehvah but did not interrupt her surprise visit with the rest of the family. Her mother's grace and compassion for others had always been Elizabeth's idea of what a true lady should mirror. It did not surprise her to see her mother busy in the kitchen; she just felt ashamed that she had not been down earlier to do it for her.

There was a little squeal on the porch, and Elizabeth ran to the door. "Give her to me, Simmy," Elizabeth called.

"You need to have one for yourself, Lizbeth."

"No, I'm just going to take yours."

"I reckon Zeb'd have a li'l say 'bout that." Simmy walked in and took over the cooking duties in the kitchen.

"Since you're cooking anyway, Simmy, I think I'll have some hot cakes, bacon, eggs, grits, and biscuits," said Anna with a smile.

"You have what I fixes." Simmy was reminding the family more and more every day of Izzy and her dry humor, and it just seemed right to them.

After breakfast, Elizabeth decided that she would approach the subject of the Arkansas visit with Papa. *No time like the present,* she thought as she followed her father into the west room.

"Papa, could I talk with you for just a moment? I would like to get your permission on something that I would really like to do with Anna."

"Come on in, school teacher."

"Papa," Elizabeth began as she took the chair right across the desk from George, "I would like to visit my cousins in Arkansas, since I didn't get to go with the family on the last visit, and I do want to meet Anna's young man, A. G."

George was quiet for a little while, looking toward the floor, seemingly in deep thought. "I know I have not been too supportive of Anna where A. G. is concerned, but she is so young, Elizabeth."

"Papa, Anna is seventeen years old—a young lady. Surely you knew that this day would come eventually." She assumed her teacher role. "I could act as chaperone, but Anna's parents raised her so well that I don't believe that she would really need one." she smiled as she looked into kind but much older eyes.

"You're right, of course, Elizabeth, and if I trust my child—and I do—I have to let her go."

"Thank you, Papa. Anna will be so pleased, and I really do think this will do wonders in helping her grow up a little more."

"Call your sister in, Elizabeth."

Anna walked into the room. "Is this a lecture? What did I do now, or was it Elizabeth this time?" She smiled at her Papa and took her seat next to Elizabeth.

"Anna, your sister and I have been talking, and she has convinced me that the two of you need to go to Arkansas for a cousin visit—and any friends of theirs that may happen to show up. I know that I promised to take you, but I'm sure you will agree that the two of you would have more fun without Mama and Papa there to pester you. What do you think?"

Anna sprang from her chair and around the desk to her father. "Papa, you are just about the best papa in the whole wide world!" Papa knew the drawl very well, but in spite of it all, he loved hearing it.

That night, as Elizabeth and Anna got ready for bed, they began to make plans for their trip to Arkansas.

"Okay, Miss Anna, you will have to give me next week to finish this thing with Mary's college, and then we will be Arkansas-bound. You'll need to write to Uncle John and Uncle Neill and tell them that we would like to come for a short visit."

"How short, Elizabeth?"

"Well, I'm not staying for a month. That would be wearing out our welcome—and besides, I have work to do at the school. You can come to Clinton on the train, and I will meet you at the depot. You can stay at Aunt Lucy's house or at the school dormitory with me in my room."

Anna wrinkled up her nose. "Not Aunt Lucy, please."

"All right, in the dorm with me. You might find it quite interesting."

"This is going to be so much fun, Elizabeth; I can hardly wait. Thank you so much for talking to Papa."

"Am I just the greatest li'l ol' sister in the whole wide world?"

Anna jumped from her bed onto Elizabeth, wrapping her in a secure bear hug and rolling onto the floor.

"Elizabeth Mae, I can't believe you mocked me like that," she said with a laugh.

"Get off me, Anna Jane, or I'll beat you senseless."

It had been many years since they had teased each other like this, and the memories of a wonderful childhood came flooding back. They were young girls once more in Tehvah. They were home together once more.

Chapter 15

Elizabeth returned to Clinton to take care of the business of trying to get Mary into a college, and Anna was happily bustling around, making her final preparations for her visit to Arkansas. She had written to A. G. to tell him the good news. Papa had stopped second-guessing his decision about letting Anna make her trip and was working on his feelings toward the young man.

Like it or not, I may as well get used to the fact that Anna will be moving to Arkansas with a husband before too long. George had all sorts of visions of life at Tehvah without both his girls, and none of them seemed too exciting. It was at times like these that George questioned the death of his only son, Hugh. There were, of course, plenty of Torrey boys living in Arkansas who would carry on the family name, but somehow it just wouldn't be the same as having a son of his own.

A. G. Kelly. George mulled this over in his mind. *That A. G. stands for Angus Gilchrist. Now if Grandma was still alive, she would work up a kinship—after all, she was a Gilchrist. That would mean the passing on of the family name. Oh, I sound just like my mother-in-law. Whatever happened to leaving it in God's hands instead of George working out the solution?* He chuckled. *Would it be so bad to have a little grandson with red, curly hair?*

His solitude was broken by the sound of Anna's voice. "Papa, have you heard from Elizabeth? I'm a little worried that she might get busy and forget her promise. I have already written to our cousins about the trip."

"Anna, I can assure you that Elizabeth has not forgotten her promise to you. Has she ever let you down before?"

Her brow wrinkled as though she was deep in thought. "Well, let me see." A little grin crossed her face.

"Anna, you were the inspiration for this whole idea your sister had of a visit to Arkansas. You should be grateful to have such a thoughtful sister."

"I know, Papa, but I'm just so anxious to see my cousins."

"Yes, Anna, I know you are."

The next day, the letter came from Elizabeth. She had enlisted the help of Miss Dickey for a recommendation for admission to a college for Mary to attend, and Mary had been accepted. Elizabeth sounded very excited as her letter went on with instructions for Anna to drive to Clinton in the buggy and stay with her in her dormitory room. From Clinton, they would go by train to Arkansas and the visit with the cousins, among others. They would leave Clinton for Arkansas in two weeks.

Anna arrived in Clinton at the appointed time, and Elizabeth met her. After a quick hug, they collected Anna's bags and made their way to the little carriage that would take them to the school.

"My goodness, Anna; look at all those bags. We aren't staying for the whole year!"

"I know, but I just couldn't make up my mind about what I wanted to wear, although I do look quite fetching in anything I put on. Don't you think?"

"Oh, you're such a modest child."

They both laughed as they drove down the long main street; past Aunt Lucy's, where they waved; and on to the school.

"I'm so glad I didn't have to stay at Aunt Lucy's house," Anna remarked as she looked at the brick dormitory in front of them.

"I know it doesn't look like the dorm on the campus at Mississippi College, but we are just getting started, you know."

Anna looked apologetically at her sister. "Elizabeth, I didn't mean to sound ungrateful; I'm just happy to be here with you. Besides, Aunt Lucy's house always smells like an old lady."

"Tell me, Anna, just how does an old lady smell?"

"You know, all powdery and musty, I guess."

"Anna Jane Torrey, you ought to be ashamed of yourself!"

"Oh, I am, Elizabeth; truly I am."

"At some point in time, you need to think in terms of growing up and becoming more serious, Anna."

That night was spent in conversations about marriage, weddings, and honeymoons, but not one word about babies.

All the students from Elizabeth's class had returned home for the summer, and Anna did not get to meet them. She got a tour of the school and a little history lesson, which included Miss Sarah Dickey and all the adversities that she overcame on her way to founding the school. Anna was impressed with her life of struggling for her education and going from family to family with promises of being provided with the opportunity for an education, but Anna's mind was more on her own life at this point. This was a story that was more endearing to Elizabeth than to Anna.

Anna gracefully endured all the history about Miss Dickey's life and the school. She tried to show great interest in the beautiful homes they visited and even a little tea and scones at Aunt Lucy's house. Elizabeth even sniffed a little as she walked into Aunt Lucy's parlor for any whiff of powder or mustiness. Anna knew what her sister was doing, and she chuckled softly as she looked at Elizabeth, scolding with her eyes.

It was late in the afternoon when the train pulled in at the Arkansas station. The sun had not yet set and painted the western sky with beautiful hues of orange, red, and yellow.

Anna pressed her face to the window. "Red skies at night, sailor's delight," she said quietly.

Elizabeth looked through the part of the window left to her. She was anxious to see this young man who had come to meet them.

Anna sat forward on her seat. "There he is, Elizabeth, standing beside the buggy!"

Elizabeth would have known him immediately. He was tall, tan, and muscular from all his hard work in the Arkansas sun. He wore dark trousers, a white shirt, and a neat black vest, but more revealing was the shock of curly red hair.

"He looks like a Greek god with red hair," Elizabeth breathed to herself.

Anna was out of her seat the instant the train rolled to a stop. Once outside, Anna crossed the dirty platform in a dainty little gait toward A. G. Her petticoats rustled as she ran, and she sprang into his arms. He caught her and swung her around in a circle, holding on tightly as if he would never let go of her. As Elizabeth stepped from the train and witnessed the sheer delight of the two wrapped in each other's embrace, she could not help being a bit envious. *I must be a fool for not looking for this kind of love.*

Anna remembered her sister and turned in her direction. "Elizabeth, this is Mr. A. G. Kelly, my wonderful beau."

Elizabeth reached for his hand. "I'm so glad to meet you, A. G. I feel that I need to tell you what a pain my little sister really is." Even in the waning light of the evening, Elizabeth could see the blush on his cheeks.

The buggy creaked as the wheels rolled over rocks and bounced along the ruts made by years of travel. Elizabeth felt like an invisible presence as A. G. and Anna chattered adoringly. For a brief moment, she wished to be in Anna's place—but for only a moment. The fleeting thought brought guilt over her envy.

The warm glow of lamps shining through the windows of both

houses was a welcome sight. Assisted by A. G., the two sisters climbed down from the buggy and greeted the Torrey family members who awaited their arrival.

"What has happened to the two little girls I used to know and love?" Uncle John approached with outstretched arms.

"They grew up!" Uncle Neill followed with the rest of the clan.

Inside the modest home of John Torrey, the girls felt the warmth and welcome. The smell of cinnamon and spice permeated the air. The ceilings in the house were not tall like the ones at Tehvah, but this gave the rooms a cozier feel. Hesitating for a moment at the door, Elizabeth tried to take in the warmth of the room so that she would be able to remember it later.

When everyone was inside, Mae brought in cups of apple cider. The steam rose from each cup, and although the day had been a warm one, the cider fit the atmosphere inside the home. As Elizabeth seated herself at the kitchen table overlaid with Mae's best white damask tablecloth, she thought of how happy Anna and A. G. were at the train depot, and she questioned her own decision to devote all her time to the school and so very little to her own needs.

What's wrong with me? she thought. *Can I continue to sacrifice those feelings for the sake of someone totally unrelated to me?* Realizing at last that she was simply caught up in the moment, she answered her own question—*Yes, yes I can!*

The days went by quickly for Anna, and it was soon time for them to return home. On the return trip home, Elizabeth noticed that Anna was not quite as sad as she had expected her to be. "Anna, you seem very quiet. I thought you would at least shed a few tears about your departure."

Anna put her head back against her seat and closed her eyes as if deep in thought. "Elizabeth, A. G. asked me to marry him, and I said yes, of course."

"What will Papa say about this, Anna?"

Anna opened her eyes and spoke very quickly. "Oh, A. G. intends to ask Papa for my hand like any proper young gentleman when he comes to Tehvah next month. I do hope Papa will cooperate."

"That's wonderful, Anna. I can hardly believe that you are old enough or wise enough to become someone's wife."

"Why, Elizabeth, I do declare, how you do go on." They both laughed once more at Anna's saccharine Southern drawl.

"Anna, you are such a clown, but I love you so much."

Chapter 16

The following month, A. G. made his trip to Tehvah, hat in hand, and requested the hand of Miss Anna Jane Torrey. Papa was civil, Elizabeth would say, knowing it was a done deal no matter what he said.

The wedding was planned for June in the little community church in town.

Certain requests were made by Anna, the first being that Mr. McEachern not be asked to pray. "Oh, Papa, we would not get out of that church for days. You know how Mr. McEachern does love to pray."

Papa would give the bride away, and Elizabeth would be the maid of honor. David Michael would serve as the best man if they could keep him from climbing the church steeple.

Flora was concerned with getting Tehvah spruced up and ready for quite a few overnight guests. "John and Mae could have an upstairs bedroom, and the one across the hall would be for Neill and Rankin. Mrs. Kelly could occupy the old nursery downstairs, and George and I will take Izzy and Simmy's old room off the kitchen. We will bring in the two cots and put all four girls in Anna's room." Flora was relieved that she had solved that problem, but she still had six boys to take care of. There were several empty cottages out back that had been unoccupied since the field hands and their families had moved out. Flora thought they could be cleaned and made ready for the boys in time for the wedding. One cottage would easily sleep three boys in comfort. She and the girls, with Simmy and Zeb's help, could handle this little chore. There was silver to clean and polishing to be done; things must be just right for Anna's big day. It would take all the time they had to complete these tasks.

Deciding to begin with the two cottages out back, Flora, the girls, Zeb, and Simmy took on the task. Flora opened the door to the Simeon house, and a wave of mold and musk escaped into the fresh air outside.

"Phew!" Anna reacted to the smell that reminded her of Aunt Lucy.

"What did you expect, Anna?" Flora asked as she stepped inside. "This is what happens to a house when nobody is in it to care for it. Someone has to come in and make it better." Flora had already begun to open the windows and doors as an avenue of escape for the dust that she knew would fill the air when the cleaning began.

"What do I do, Mama?" Anna looked around aimlessly.

"Well, praise be; this is what I get for not teaching my girls to take on more responsibility." Flora handed Anna a dusting cloth and a broom. "Take your pick, missy. Sweep or dust."

To Flora's great delight, two of the field hands' wives came into the little cottage. One carried a pail in her hand and the second a scrub brush.

Anna was sneezing daintily, and Elizabeth was eyeing her with disdain. "Come on, Miss Anna; it's your wedding, so the least you can do is to help out a little."

Anna blew the dust from her nose into her little handkerchief and replaced it in her pocket. "All right, Elizabeth; I'm ready to *scrub!*"

Zeb took the mattresses from the beds and placed them outside on a table to air in the bright sunshine while Anna and Simmy swept the floor and polished the wooden furniture. Feeling good about her efforts, Anna began to hum a little song.

"Why, Anna, you might just make it as a good housewife after all." Elizabeth was watching her younger sister with much interest and surprise.

"I knew I *could* do it; I had just never tried."

The floor scrubbing took the longest, and then rinsing off the lye soap took a while, but after about three and a half hours, the floors shone. Flora left the windows open to the breeze, and as she closed the door to the first cottage, she could smell the clean of the soap and the fragrant lilac flowers that Anna had picked for the table in the little kitchen. "Job well done," Flora announced as they walked back to the main house.

Anna walked a little slower than usual on aching feet. "If the boys don't want to stay there, the girls will, 'cause it sure smells a lot better than our room, Elizabeth."

"Yes, it does!" Elizabeth laughed as she put an arm around her sister's drooping shoulder.

After lunch, the two girls climbed the stairs wearily to take a little rest before tackling the next project. Elizabeth fell across her bed and closed her eyes. Anna sat on her bed, facing Elizabeth's direction. "I know I should be a little tired, but I just keep thinking about A. G., and I just can't slow down my mind."

"Anna, I need rest. If you can't slow down your mind, could you at least slow down your mouth?"

"Sorry, I'll be quiet."

In no time at all, Elizabeth was fast asleep. Looking for something to read, Anna saw a sheet of paper in one of Elizabeth's books. *Maybe she has a beau after all,* Anna thought to herself as she slipped the paper from the book. She convinced herself that Elizabeth would not mind as she unfolded the paper. It revealed a beautiful poem written in Elizabeth's hand.

It was just a little olive tree that stood upon a hill,
No bigger than a child of twelve was tall.

Nothing much to look at as you passed it in the day,
It was brown and bare when leaves began to fall.

The people in the town below would often pass that way
And stop and rest beneath its shade as they traveled in the day.

Never once a thank you for the comfort they had found,
Though they ate the fruit in season as they sat upon the ground.

As years went by, the branches grew where birds could build their nest.
And more than one could sit below and take a shady rest.

Still never once a thank you for the melodies they heard.
Through all its years of service, no one ever said a word.

Then one day, a woodsman came and chopped the big tree down.
No one seemed to really care that it lay upon the ground.

But soon the tree was seen once more as it stood upon a hill.
It was on a Friday evening, and all the world was still.

The figure of a man was there upon that olive tree,
And people 'neath its shadow crowded close so they could see.

The tree was now a cruel cross that men had fashioned there.
The shame of what they did that day is pain we all must bear.

Why He prayed for their forgiveness, not a one of them had guessed,
But on that day, a price was paid, and the olive tree was blessed.

Tears filled Anna's eyes as she looked at her sleeping sister and thought, *This is what you are about, Elizabeth. If everyone loved the Lord as sincerely as you and Papa, we would all be the better for it.* She quietly replaced the poem where she had found it in the book. Anna felt a little guilty that she had read Elizabeth's very personal and beautiful poem without her permission. Yet Anna had a newfound respect for her sister and all her compassion and sincerity.

With all the work to be done before Anna's wedding, Flora had to accept the fact that she simply did not have the time to make Anna a wedding dress. "Anna, we will have to go to New Orleans and buy a dress. Papa has given us his permission. It will be a nice trip for us to make—just us girls."

New Orleans was exciting and beautiful. Anna and Elizabeth had never been to the city but had heard about the Mardi Gras and the general reputation of the city's inhabitants. "I heard that the city is almost all Catholic, and their morals are pretty lax." Anna's heels made a clicking sound on the cobblestones.

"Anna, all Catholics don't have loose morals. They pray often and have great compassion for others." Elizabeth felt that her sister was being a bit judgmental.

"My friend told me that they could commit a sin, and all they had to do was go to a priest and confess to him, and they'd be forgiven."

"Anna, I think that there must be a little more to it than that."

Flora hailed a horse-drawn cab, and the three climbed in for a short ride to a little rooming house on Royal Street. After paying the cabby, the three got out and walked toward a courtyard inside a wrought iron fence. Inside the gate were small palms and a few citrus trees. "Everything is so lush and green," Anna said, impressed with the size of the flowers that grew on the citrus trees.

"It rains often in New Orleans," Elizabeth told her. "That more than likely accounts for the phenomenal growth rate of these plants."

Hanging baskets were abundant on the French-style balconies

above the courtyard, and were filled with petunias and begonias in shades of purple and red. There was a little fountain in the center of the garden, and the sound of the trickling water was very soothing. As Anna inspected the fountain more closely, she became quite excited. Placing her hands on the edge of the cool, ceramic pool, she spoke softly, "There are huge goldfish in here!" She did not wish people to think that she was ignorant about New Orleans fish pools.

Flora interrupted, "Let's get settled into our room and then look for Madam Rene's dress shop. It is within walking distance of this court."

After settling into the cozy little room and opening the doors leading to the balcony, the women unpacked their bags and headed once again for the cobblestone streets of New Orleans. Madam Rene's shop was nearby in a brick building that was very narrow in the front but extended back a long way. The dresses were a perfusion of color, and the shop smelled of candle wax and bath salts. Anna easily found the section devoted to the white gowns and was as excited as a child in a candy store. She moved through the satin, lace, silk, and tulle. Holding each favorite up in front of her, she gazed longingly into the full-length mirror. "Oh, how can I decide on one of these? They are all so very beautiful."

"That's why we came with you—so you won't buy out the store," Elizabeth answered.

"Oh, Mama, look at this one!" Anna chose a long white satin dress with a high collar and tiny buttons in the front. Little brocade roses were scattered over the bodice, and the back laced corset was fashioned with white silk ribbon that cascaded down. Anna had a very small waist, like her mother, and this dress would accent that ladylike feature.

Anna tried on the dress, and it needed no alterations. It fit Anna as though it had been made for her. They paid for the dress and took it with them. As the women walked back to the French Quarter, Anna held on to the box as if she expected someone to take it from her.

Anna walked slightly behind the two others. "Did you notice the smell in Miss Rene's shop?"

"Why do you have this obsession with odors, Anna?" Elizabeth was curious.

"I'm not obsessed, Elizabeth, just curious. When I marry A. G. and we have a home, my house is going to smell fresh, like Simeon cottage."

"Well," Flora offered, "that takes hard work and cleaning on a regular basis."

Elizabeth laughed. "You think you could do that, Anna?"

"I truly believe I could. I do declare, Elizabeth, you think of me as completely helpless." Anna sounded somewhat serious, but she drawled in fun for the benefit of Elizabeth.

"Can we just hurry along, Anna, before I lose my breakfast right here on Royal Street?"

Back at Tehvah, the three ladies were pleased with their shopping trip to New Orleans. While Flora broke the good news of what a bargain the dress was, Anna unpacked the dress and tried it on once again just to make sure it still fit.

"Maybe I'll show it to Papa, Elizabeth. I really would like to get his opinion."

"Anna, are you sure you're not just fishing for a compliment from Papa?"

"Elizabeth, you can be so mean sometimes."

"I just don't think that this would be the best time to show it to Papa. Right now, Mama is breaking the news to him of how much it cost, and he might be in shock. Wait and get his reaction on your wedding day." Anna made a clapping motion with her hands, signaling her approval of Elizabeth's idea.

The girls heard Simmy call as she climbed the stairs to the girls' room.

"Bring her to *me*," Elizabeth called to Simmy before she had reached the top of the stairs.

"She not with me." Simmy entered the room alone. Elizabeth was disappointed that she wouldn't get to hold little Izzy but knew that young children and stairs were always a dangerous combination.

"Come see my dress, Simmy!" Anna was excited to hear what Simmy would have to say.

"You looks happy as I did when Miss Flora give me that white dress on my birthday."

"I am happy, Simmy. I know how you feel about Zeb now. Isn't it wonderful?"

"'Deed it is. What I wants to do is to make you a li'l crown of flowers for your hair. Iffin you got any extra lace, I can make it mighty pretty."

"That's a wonderful idea, Simmy. I'd be honored to have you make my veil. I got one in New Orleans, but I really don't like the way it looks with my dress. There is tulle on it that you can use."

Simmy's smile was as big that day as it was the day they played beside the creek. "You gone like it, I know. I can make one you be proud of, Anna."

As Anna gave her expensive New Orleans veil to Simmy, she hugged her. "I know I'll love it. You are my best friend, and I love you."

Simmy turned, walking to the door. "I needs to get the vines for the crown right now and weave 'em so as they has time to dry 'fore to put the flowers on."

With Simmy safely down the stairs, Elizabeth looked lovingly at her little sister.

"Anna, you never cease to amaze me. Just when I think you are the most self-centered person in the world, you go and do something terrific like that."

Anna almost reverted back to her old "Well, I do declare ..." but this did not seem to call for levity. She simply answered, "Thank you. Coming from you, that means a lot. You know that Simmy is my best friend, but you have always been my hero."

Chapter 17

The wedding day drew near, but time went by too slowly for Anna. With only days before the big day, all seemed ready. The cottages had been cleaned, and Anna made sure that fresh flowers were always on the tables because of her obsession with smells. The silver had been polished, Tehvah was given a fresh coat of paint, and the inside was cleaned top to bottom. An exhausted Flora climbed the stairs to the girls' room and addressed Anna.

"Anna, when you say 'till death us do part' in your vows, you better mean it, because the work done by everyone here has been incomparable."

Anna ran to her mother and hugged her tightly. "I know, Mama, and I don't know how I could ever thank everyone. You don't have to worry about doing this again unless Elizabeth changes her mind."

Elizabeth grinned. She had already chosen her path in life, and unless the Lord threw a stumbling block in front of her to get her attention, this was what she had chosen. She could not even imagine loving a man the way Anna loved A. G.

They all went downstairs together and met Simmy as she came through the back door. "'Fore you ask, Miss Lizabeth, Izzy not with me. Zeb got her, and I got a headband for Anna."

Simmy brought her hidden hand out in front of her to expose a delicately woven crown with tulle and ribbons falling elegantly in the back. "I gotta wait to put on the flowers or they be wilted."

"Oh, Simmy, I knew that it would be pretty, but I never expected all this elegance. I could have looked for a year and never found anything so lovely." When Anna saw all the delicate stitching Simmy did on the veil, her eyes filled to the brim with grateful tears. "How can I ever thank you, Simmy?"

"You my friend, Anna, and that's enough."

Flora took the crown and placed it on Anna's head. "It fits you perfectly. Simmy, you need to open your own shop and sell these little gems to the public."

Simmy had not stopped smiling since she came into the room. She was relieved that Anna liked her veil. "It be lookin' real good with the flowers all around." Simmy was already on her way to the door, satisfied that Anna really was pleased with her labor of love.

Two days later, the Torrey kin began to arrive. Just the sound of all the voices and laughter made the occasion better. The boys were shown their sleeping quarters, and they were very pleased with everything except the flowers Anna had placed on the table. David immediately went to the back porch, where he could see the woods. "Hey," he said, "I didn't know you had any woods in Mississippi."

Uncle George, who was standing near with John and Neil, replied, "How else do you suppose I learned to outshoot your paw and uncle?"

John's comment was short. "Oh, that's really a good one, George." They laughed as they headed back to Tehvah, where the ladies were busy discussing the sleeping arrangements and the details of the wedding.

"Sounds like a henhouse in here." George walked in with his cousins. Elizabeth could not remember the last time she had heard her father joking and looking so completely happy.

"Papa, you know you love that cackling sound."

"Yes, I do, Elizabeth; it's the sound of family having a great old time."

Flora took the two wives upstairs and showed them where they would sleep.

Rankin looked at the spacious room with the little balcony, heavy bed, and shiny bureau, and she loved it almost as much as Elizabeth had the coziness of her own modest home.

"Oh, Flora, it is so dignified—fit for a queen."

Elizabeth, who had accompanied them upstairs, put her arm around Rankin's waist, "You *are* a queen, Aunt Rankin."

The process was repeated until everyone was given sleeping arrangements. The girls were most happy to be together in one room and immediately began to talk about the wedding.

Mrs. Kelly was impressed with Tehvah and her very own room. A. G. had been with the boys for a while, but when the chance presented itself, he was out the door, looking for Anna. They walked hand-in-hand toward the little creek in the back. Seeing them from the window on the side of the house, Elizabeth called, "Do you need a chaperone? I could help you look for snakes."

Anna turned to look at Elizabeth, and seeing her head in the window, poked her tongue out at her sister.

Pulling her head back inside the window, Elizabeth looked at her cousins. "Guess not," she said.

That night, everyone helped with the supper. Flora had put her best foot forward with the cooking, even though she had quite a bit of help. The table was covered with food and the side table with desserts. Flora had figured on food for twenty with a little extra, because she had never really cooked for boys and had no idea how much food boys could consume. There were two big hams, four baked chickens, a deer tenderloin, and pork chops. The vegetables included almost every type of vegetable from the garden, and Simmy even made corn bread the way Izzy had made it. There were cakes, pecan and sweet potato pies, and jam mixed with sweet cream to top the buttermilk cake.

When everyone walked into the dining room, Neill remarked, "It looks like you are feeding a regiment of Confederate soldiers, Flora."

"She is, dear brother, she is." John laughed and sat down.

The meal was a belt-popping success, as John would later call it. Since there was not enough room for everyone at the dining room table, some of the boys took their plates into the kitchen.

The day of the wedding finally arrived, and Anna was becoming nervous about her veil. "I wonder if Simmy has finished my veil." And as if by magic, Simmy appeared at the door of the kitchen, veil in hand.

"I got myself up early this mornin' and picked the flowers for your veil. I want them to be fresh."

Anna looked lovingly at the delicate blossoms tucked neatly into the crown of the veil. There were sprigs of bridal wreath with tiny white petals all up and down the stem, bright yellow forsythia, and tiny pink Cherokee roses. "I love it, Simmy. Thank you so much. It really completes my day." Pleased that Anna liked her creation and having completed her task, Simmy left to get herself ready for the big event.

Flora piled Anna's hair up on her head in a bouffant with some dark curls cascading down the back. Anna slipped on her dress, which Elizabeth laced up in the back, and pinched her cheeks for some color. Now the veil would go on.

"My goodness, Anna, I have never seen you look so beautiful." Flora looked at her daughter through tears and continued, "I think maybe we had better let your father have a look at this before the wedding, or he may not make it through the ceremony."

"Make sure that A. G. is not around to see me."

Flora walked down the stairs and called up to Anna, "He has already left for the church."

Anna walked down the steps and into the hall, where she could see her father waiting. He seemed different as he looked at her over his wire-framed glasses. This time, he was not looking at a little girl but at a beautiful, grown young lady. His eyes glistened with tears that he was unable to control. Anna ran to him as she did in times past and whispered, "Papa, I love you."

The church was filled with family and friends, and as promised,

Mr. McEachern was not asked to pray. It was a sweet ceremony, and to Anna's surprise, the pastor did not make it a five-point sermon or even a two-pointer. He just married the two of them, and after they said "I do," everyone went back to Tehvah for cake and punch.

Tehvah was decorated with magnolia leaves and bridal wreath, and to Anna's great delight, Mama had put rosemary and lilacs in the floral arrangements strictly for the smell.

The dining table was set with a huge arrangement of spring flowers in the center of an Irish lace tablecloth. Wedding cake baked by Flora, with the help of Rankin and Mae, and a large silver punch bowl decorated around the base with rosemary from Flora's herb garden completed the table. The plates, teacups, and napkins were set on the side table, making it easier for the guests to partake of the food.

The guests filled the house, being very careful to compliment Flora's hard work.

Anna received her guests and went upstairs to change her clothes and retrieve her bag for the trip she and A. G. would make to New Orleans for the honeymoon.

The boys had tied ribbon streamers to the back of the horse-drawn buggy and even a big bow around the horse's neck. A. G. and Anna left Tehvah and climbed into the buggy, forgetting the luggage on the ground. Zeb had been asked by Anna to drive them to the station, and he smiled at their excitement, picked up the luggage, and climbed into the driver's seat.

Everybody waved their good-byes. The guests left, and everyone else went back into the house to begin the long, arduous task of cleaning up after the reception.

Mae looked around at the once-spotless dining room cluttered with little plates covered with cake crumbs and punch cups with napkins tucked inside. The children who attended were, for the most part, very well-behaved, and there were very few crumbs or spills on the polished floor.

"It was a beautiful wedding," Rankin remarked as she collected plates and cups around the room.

"I thought it went off very smoothly," added Mary Kelly, who was very proud that her son was now married to a young lady whom she dearly loved. She had considered the Gilchrist last name and mentioned to Flora, whose maiden name was Gilchrist, that she sincerely hoped the two were not related. Flora closed her eyes for just a short moment and thought, *If they are, it's too late now to worry about it.*

The work seemed to go by quickly as the ladies talked and genuinely enjoyed one another's company. The dishes were washed and returned to the cupboard once more. The floors were swept and lightly mopped to remove any cake or punch residue that was left on the floor by careless guests.

The ladies went out to the cottages to survey the damage that might have been done by the boys. When she walked into Simeon cottage, Mae was very surprised to see that the boys had packed their bags and left the cottage just as it had been when they first came, except for the flowers on the table. Those had been removed.

"Will wonders never cease?" Mae exclaimed. "I need to leave the boys over here for a while longer."

"They are very nice boys, Mae," Flora assured her.

"Mae, I would appreciate it so very much if you and Rankin would keep a motherly eye on Anna. I know they will live close to you there in Arkansas, and I still perceive Anna as a child. She still has so much growing up to do, and I would feel so much better knowing that she had someone to talk to and give her advice on important things."

"Flora, that child is family. You *know* that we will be close by to help out in any situation," Rankin assured her.

"Well, speaking of Arkansas," Mae added, "I guess it's about time for us to get to the station, or we will miss our train, and I know you don't need this much company for one day longer. You and George need to make a trip to Arkansas, since Elizabeth will be away at school, and you have Zeb right here on the place to see things run smoothly."

"It's hard to get George away from this place, but I don't know of any place he would rather be, especially now that Anna will be living there."

As Mae walked out the cottage door, she asked Flora, "Do you think that Elizabeth will ever marry?"

"I think that Elizabeth has her own agenda on trying to contribute to making the world a better place, and until she feels led to do something different, that will be the primary goal in her life."

"Can't argue with that kind of dedication." Mae started upstairs to the bedroom for her bag. "I can't tell you how much we enjoyed our stay," she said. "If I had known you had so much room, I'd have come sooner."

"You know you are always welcome."

The first of the week, the honeymooners returned to Arkansas from New Orleans. "Still like ol' A. G.?" Richard asked as he picked them up at the depot. "What'd you bring me, a voodoo doll dressed like David?"

"No," shouted A. G., "you're so rich and popular, you don't need anything, but I brought David a snake!"

They both laughed. Richard drove the two to the Kelly place and a little house that A. G. had been working on ever since he had met Anna.

"It's not Tehvah, but we can add on to it."

Anna smiled at A. G. "I don't need a Tehvah, A. G. All I want is you."

"That's sure a poor trade," Richard said with a laugh.

"Can't you be serious for one minute?" A. G. sounded a bit agitated.

"I am serious," Richard replied with a laugh.

Anna wrinkled up her nose at Richard and climbed down from

the buggy. A. G. swept her up in his arms and carried her across the threshold of her new home.

"Guess this is where I'm supposed to leave," Richard said as he turned the buggy toward home.

"At least you got something right," called A. G. as he went inside and closed the door.

Chapter 18

It was a bleak day in December as Elizabeth sat in her dorm room, a pile of papers on the desk in front of her. She was correcting test papers and smiling, as she could see the progress of her students. It was evident to her that they enjoyed their classes, especially Elizabeth's favorite, literature. She was pleased at how far they had come with their understanding and use of grammar. She thought of Mary, who had gone away to attend college, and how proud she was to hear from one of her professors on the progress Mary was making.

I knew she could do it! Elizabeth thought. She recalled past events and could see a controlling hand in all that had transpired. *It's strange how you can't see the good in things until you get older.*

That evening, she received a letter from her mother.

Dear Elizabeth,

I hope that this letter finds you well. Things at Tehvah are going well. Little Izzy is growing by leaps and bounds and keeps me occupied enough so that I don't miss my own girls as much. She talks about "Izbeff" often, and I know that she misses you.

Yesterday, Simmy took her to the edge of the creek, where she allowed Izzy to squash her toes in the mud the way you three girls used to do, and she squealed in pure delight.

Papa has been feeling poorly of late, but I believe it is from too much work and not enough rest. I talked to Dr. Buie, and he gave me some medicine for a cough he has been having. I feel sure that he will be his old self soon.

I got a short letter from Anna last week, and they are all doing well. She is still as happy as a clam, but no babies yet. We need to all go to Arkansas and visit with her and see if she has picked up any pointers on cooking and cleaning from her mother-in-law.

Elizabeth put the letter on the desk in front of her as she remembered moments with Anna from their childhood and the fun and antics they shared. She remembered the episode at the creek with Simmy and the mud, the turtle attacks, the hanging tree, and the little cemetery at the back of Tehvah. Picking the letter up once again, she thought, *I really must be getting old.*

I hope you are planning on coming home for Christmas, because we all miss you very much. Anna and A. G. will be here the week of Christmas, so plan on lots of late-night talks and a lot of laughter. Simmy and Zeb are looking forward to seeing you as well as little Izzy.

There is a new family in town, and they have an unmarried son just about your age. I'm not suggesting anything—just that he is very nice and quite handsome. Think about it.

Much love,

Mama

Elizabeth put down the letter with a smile. *If Anna doesn't have a baby soon, Mama is going to drive me crazy about meeting someone and getting married.*

The week of Christmas arrived. It was crisp and windy, but there was no snow. It seldom snowed in Mississippi, so Elizabeth supposed it would be a typical Mississippi Christmas. As she packed her bag for her trip home, she wondered if her mother would invite any new neighbors over for the holidays. How embarrassing that would be.

A school worker took Elizabeth to the depot, and Elizabeth felt very excited about going home for Christmas. As the train rolled along, Elizabeth peered out the window, watching the familiar landscape of tall pines and oak trees go by like giants running in the opposite direction. The wind waved the smaller branches at her, and she smiled to think that she had imagined such a childlike picture.

Her eyes were intent on the scenery passing by in an almost hypnotic way. It took the toot of the train whistle to snap her back to the present, and she noticed the small white flakes that filled the air. She sat straight up in her seat and squinted at the scene. *It's snowing!* she thought, and she looked around at the other passengers to see if they were as excited as she. *I can't wait to see Tehvah in the snow! Maybe if it gets cold enough, the creek will freeze. No, that's never happened before—besides, my old turtle buddies will get awfully cold.*

The train pulled into the station, and Elizabeth looked out the window to see Zeb in a heavy coat, waiting in the buggy to take her home to Tehvah and Mama and Papa. She felt just like a little child again, trembling half from the icy wind and half with the pure excitement of being home.

Zeb helped her from the train, and she gave him a big hug. Lifting her bags into the buggy, he said, "Miss Elizabeth, it sure good to see you." They climbed into the buggy, and in no time at all, they were at Tehvah. Elizabeth was home.

Mama had decorated the house with fir boughs along the railings of the porch, fir limbs over and around the door, and brightly glowing candles in each window. Inside the parlor was the big Christmas tree, decorated with red bows, candles, and the familiar, beautiful old angel sitting on the very top of the tree. The smell of cloves and cinnamon simmering on the stove filled the hall and all the rooms, as in Christmases past.

"Mama," Elizabeth called. Flora appeared from the kitchen, looking older but just as beautiful as she always had.

"Oh, Elizabeth, let me look at you. You look so thin, but I can fix that up this week."

Elizabeth embraced her mother, and the two walked toward the kitchen. "When will Anna be here, Mama?"

"I'm thinking sometime tomorrow. Yes, it will be tomorrow," her mother answered.

"I can't believe I'm home, and it's snowing to boot." Elizabeth kissed her mother and went immediately to the west room to see Papa.

The next morning, Elizabeth came downstairs and felt that she had gone back in time when she saw the ham, eggs, grits, and big plate of hot biscuits on the side table.

"Well, 'bout time you crawled out of bed, Miss Lazy Bones." The familiar voice of Simmy came from the kitchen. Elizabeth ran into the kitchen and threw her arms around her old friend.

"Oh, Simmy, you remind me so much of Izzy, and I surely hope you can cook half as well as she did."

"That don't happen, Missy. You lucky I come out on this cold day."

"Is it still snowing, Simmy?"

"Iffin it ain't, the cotton come in early and be blowin' all over the place."

"Where is my baby, Simmy?

"It too cold for her to get out."

"Well, I'll just have the brave the cold and go to her. Simmy, when I went in to see Papa, he didn't look like he felt too good. How long has he been feeling like this?"

"He been poorly 'bout a week or so."

It was snowing hard in Arkansas as Anna and A. G. climbed aboard the train for Mississippi. To Anna's surprise, it was still snowing as the train pulled into the station at home. Zeb was there with the buggy to meet them.

"Good ol' Zeb," Anna said. "I don't know what Papa would do without him."

With each step came a crunch as Anna walked in the snow toward the buggy. *What a strange sight in the state of Mississippi,* she thought.

The buggy pulled into the front yard of Tehvah, and Anna looked at the snow covering her old home and the yard. The tree limbs were covered with so much snow that it seemed to Anna they may break at any time. Somehow, this snow was even more beautiful than the Arkansas snow, and Anna smiled as she tried to understand why she had that feeling. She jumped to the ground and ran to the door. Bursting into the house, she called, "Papa, Mama, Elizabeth, I'm home! Home from the hills."

A clatter of footsteps quickly descended the stairs. Elizabeth bounded down the steps and grabbed her younger sister. "How I've longed to see you," she said as she squeezed Anna.

"I never thought I'd hear that!" Anna teased.

Mama came down the hall to greet her daughter with a hug.

"Where is Papa?" Anna thought he would be the first to greet her.

"He's been feeling a bit poorly, and I believe he is upstairs, taking a short nap. Go up and see him," Mama said with a smile.

"No need to come and get me," Papa called. "I'm on my way down. Did I hear my little Anna?"

"Well," said Mama, "you two are the best medicine he has had all week."

"Where is A. G.?" Papa asked.

"Right here, Mr. Torrey. I thought it best not to get between these two."

"Smart man."

The sun rose the next morning and glistened on the deep white snow. Elizabeth and Anna were up by six, drinking their coffee and looking out the kitchen window at the beauty of the land all dressed in white. The little cottages with the smoke rising skyward from the chimneys looked cozy and warm under their white blankets. At the edge of the woods, a large white-tail deer with a massive rack of at least eight points was walking cautiously toward the frozen garden.

"Everyone seems to be enjoying the snow." Elizabeth was still thrilled about the snow. "Anna, let's get our coats and walk down to the creek to see if it's frozen over!"

"Have you lost your mind, Elizabeth? It must be below zero out there!"

"Oh, you little scaredy-cat, it only gets that cold in Alaska."

"You couldn't drag me out there. Cold weather isn't good for your skin. It causes wrinkles, you know."

"Why Miss Anna, it wouldn't dare to harm your delicate skin!"

"Are you mocking me, Elizabeth?"

"Why, mercy me—no, Miss Anna. Would I be so unkind as to make fun of my lovely little Southern belle of a sister?"

Elizabeth laughed as Anna picked up a large wooden spoon and chased her sister around the kitchen.

Christmas morning arrived all too soon for the Torrey clan, because it meant that they would be leaving soon. The presents were beautifully wrapped and under the tree. Mama lit the candles again—probably for the last time that year. The family gathered around the tree. Zeb and Simmy were invited but wanted to enjoy little Izzy as she found what Santa left for her under the tree. Elizabeth and Anna realized for the first time that they had both bought a doll for Izzy.

"That's all right," Mama said. "As I seem to remember, a little girl can't have too many baby dolls. She will love them."

Anna thought that her Papa looked tired and older than the last time she was home but smiled sweetly at him as she handed him her

Christmas present. "Goodness, what a nice vest," Papa said as he tore the paper away to reveal his gift.

"That's to make up for the one I got hoe cake grease on some years back."

"Why, yes, I seem to remember something like that."

Elizabeth gave him a nice leather case for his wire-frame glasses and a pair of gold cuff links. Mama got a pretty white blouse from Elizabeth and a petticoat from Anna.

Anna received a nice cookbook and tortoise shell combs for her curly hair, while Elizabeth got a book of poems by Longfellow and her own copy of *Leaves of Grass*.

A. G. was thrilled with his new hunting cap that would cover his ears. It was a lovely Christmas for them all, but the best part was the fact that they were all together once again.

The next morning, they all left—Elizabeth for school in Clinton and Anna and A. G. for Arkansas. It did not seem to take near as long to get home as it had to reach Tehvah. Both girls worried about Papa's weakened condition but made Simmy promise to keep them posted on his progress. They both knew that she would respect their wishes. They had never imagined that Papa could get sick—or even old, for that matter. They had to face the reality of both their parents growing older and at some point dying.

I won't even think of that, Anna thought. *My Papa will get better, and we will have many more visits.* Anna smiled as she thought of her Papa.

Chapter 19

December melted into another year, and the air warmed. The earth was alive with green and early daffodils. Work in the Arkansas fields was much longer and harder, since Richard and George had moved to Oklahoma, where they heard of gold being discovered on the land occupied by the Nez Perce Indians. Shortly after they left, the Indians, under the leadership of Chief Joseph, went to war with the federal government over the shrinkage of their reservation land. John and Mae were concerned about the safety of their children. The Great West offered land and opportunity for riches to many hard-working folks. This area embraced plains, mountains, and deserts but was also the home of the Indians. Just three years earlier, General George Custer and his troops were crushed by Sioux Indians at the battle of Little Big Horn. There was unrest among all the tribes in the western states. Neill and Rankin felt that Richard and George's safety was more important than any gold or land they might find. John and Mae's son, Angus, had married his childhood sweetheart and purchased land only a short distance from their home.

Anna and A. G. were content to live in their own little house beside Mary Kelly and her family. "You can hardly blame the Indians for their actions." Anna had been thinking about all the Indian uprisings. "They have been moved off land that was theirs for hundreds of years and had their families butchered by soldiers. That Yankee general said that the only good Indian was a dead one. Actions like those at Sand Creek are worse than slavery."

A. G. sat at the little kitchen table, drinking a lukewarm cup of coffee. "I don't know, Anna. I just don't know when all the violence will stop, but it seems to continue. We have left our basic love for others and turned to … I don't know what."

"I do," Anna replied. "Everyone is greedy for something. It may be land or money or power or anything we want and feel we don't have. I don't think it will ever change." She replenished A. G.'s cup with steaming coffee and sat down at the table.

The rustling of footsteps interrupted their conversation, and David Michael appeared at the door. He had grown as a teenager and become very handsome. He had very dark eyes and brown hair that nearly reached his shoulders.

"When you gonna cut that hair, Michael?"

"When you shave off that gosh-awful beard, A. G. You saving' it to use as camouflage when you go huntin'?"

Anna bowed her head slightly so that A. G. would not see the hint of a smile that she could not control. She had been trying to convince A. G. to shave the beard, because in her opinion, he had let it get too long. She thought it looked unkempt—and besides that, it was red.

"Is Mama all right?"

"Why do you ask that, A. G.? We live hollering distance."

"It's just that you don't visit us very much—formally, I mean."

"Well, I was thinking about something, and I sort of wanted to get your opinion."

A. G. laughed. "Well, don't hold back. You never asked for my opinion before. Must be mighty important."

Undeterred by his brother's comment, Michael continued. "I was thinking about maybe joining the Torrey boys to find us some new land or maybe striking it rich. Here in Arkansas, we won't ever have anything except hard work and rocky soil. I guess I just want something better for Mama and me."

A. G. wanted to yell at Michael but realized that was not the right approach to take. "Have you asked Mama what she thinks about this move?"

"Not yet. She probably won't approve."

"First off, Michael, our mama is a pretty wise lady, and we ought to respect her opinion. If you remember, we haven't even heard from Richard and George in months and are not even sure where they are now. I really don't think Mama would approve of you taking off for parts unknown, looking for folks you may not be able to find."

"Why don't you wait until things calm down out there? By that time, we will probably have heard from the boys." Anna was trying not to interfere but was concerned with Michael's desire to go west.

"What would Mama do without you to help out on the farm?" A. G. approached the advice from a different direction, knowing how close Michael and his mother were.

"I just want to do something to give Mama a better and easier life."

"I know," replied A. G., "but let's put our heads together and figure the best way to do it."

"Stay for lunch," Anna invited. "I'm cooking dumplings."

"Thanks, Anna, but I have lots of work left to do." Michael had eaten Anna's dumplings before.

Anna stomped her foot at Michael. "You don't like my cooking," she said.

"It's not that exactly," he replied. "I just can't eat your dumplings." He jumped from the porch to the yard as Anna threw her stirring spoon at him.

"What's wrong with my cooking?" She turned to face A. G. with a frown on her face.

"It's fine, Anna. I eat it, don't I?"

"That's only because you'd starve if you didn't." In an attempt to get her mind off Michael's comment while he escaped with his life, he offered a suggestion. "Why don't you get out that cookbook your mama gave you for Christmas and try a recipe in there?"

Anna immediately fell silent and glared at her husband.

Oh, no, A. G. thought. *I think I just turned the wrong corner.* "I'd better go out and see that the cow gets milked." A. G. backed toward the door.

"That might be the best thing you could do," was Anna's only response. She plopped heavily into a chair at the little table and cupped her chin in her hands. Suddenly the scowl disappeared from her face as she recalled the day Izzy made the hoe cakes at Tehvah. Anna saw her make them so many times and could recall the process clearly. She retrieved a large mixing bowl from the cupboard, intent on duplicating the mix she had watched Izzy make so many times.

I don't need the stupid cookbook, she thought. *I've got my memory.* Anna poured cornmeal, salt, and baking powder in the bowl in amounts comparable to the ones she could recall. She took a pinch or two of sugar from the little blue and white bowl on the kitchen table and at last added the egg and enough milk to make a thin batter. Lard went into a hot skillet on the wood-burning stove, and when it melted, she poured some into her hoe cake batter.

"Dear Lord, please let me make good hoe cakes," she prayed. With the skillet just beginning to smoke, Anna dropped her first spoonful of hoe cake batter. She watched as the golden crust began to form around the edges and the wonderful aroma of the hoe cakes she used to smell coming from the kitchen at Tehvah filled the air. Her heart began to pound faster as she carefully turned them with her spoon. She placed her platter near the stove to transfer the now-golden grown, crispy delights. She dropped in another batch and turned to the platter. She pinched off an end of one of the hot cakes, and her mind returned to Tehvah and Papa's white shirt. The taste did not disappoint, and Anna almost cried with the feeling of pride that she had. "A. G.," she called, "I need you to come here now!"

Fearing that Anna was in distress, A. G. ran to the house. "Anna, what's wrong?"

Not answering, Anna smugly handed him a hot hoe cake. "Eat," she said.

A little confused, A. G. took the hoe cake and bit off a little corner. "Anna, it's delicious! I'll call Michael, because he would never believe it."

"You do that," she said proudly. She may not be able to roast a turkey, but she sure knew how to make a hoe cake.

The following year, Anna found out that she was pregnant, and the baby would be due in March of 1879. Anna would be twenty-four when the baby was born. Living up in the foothills of the mountains, it was difficult to get a doctor to arrive in time to deliver a baby. It was for this reason that A. G. looked into finding the closest midwife to aid in Anna's delivery of the child.

There was great excitement in the Kelly and the Torrey families over the news of a baby. Michael, who had forgotten all about a life of adventure, consorted with A. G. on plans to make a cradle for the new family member. "It needs to rock," said Michael.

"We can always put rockers on it. I just want it to be pretty and comfortable."

"A. G., you talk like it's gonna be a little girl. We don't want no frilly, pretty crib for a boy!"

Mary Kelly helped Anna with the nursery. The little room was painted a soft white. Anna had hoped for a pretty wallpaper but did not know what kind until the baby arrived. She didn't want a flowery print if it was a boy, so the wall treatment stopped with the neutral color.

The months went by quickly, and Anna got bigger. A. G. grew right along with her on his steady diet of fried hoe cakes. Her new love for cooking finally grew to include peas, which she cooked quite well, and fried okra. As in China, where the staple food was rice, in the Kelly household, it was hoe cakes.

Late in her pregnancy, Anna began to have problems with water retention, and A. G. made her stay in bed for most of each day. Anna missed cleaning her home, which she had begun to take great pride in, and her attempts at new recipes. She was beginning to cook very tasty dishes, and A. G. was very proud of her accomplishments along this line.

"I have talked with Mrs. Crary about being a midwife for you when delivery time comes. She is not far, and I could have her here in ten minutes or so."

"Maybe if you could fly, A. G." Anna laughed. She knew that he was trying to set her mind at ease about having someone there who was familiar with delivering babies.

"I'll have your mama here, A.G., the Torreys, and hopefully my mama. I haven't mentioned that to you, but I didn't think you would mind. It would mean a lot to me to have Mama here."

"I think your papa might enjoy being here for the birth of his first grandchild, too." A. G. smiled when he saw the look of delight on Anna's face at his suggestion.

"A. G.," Anna began, "I want you to write and invite them. You know how they both feel about imposing."

A. G. decided to sit down and write to them so they would have plenty of time to get everything at Tehvah taken care of so that they could leave for several weeks.

Dear Mr. and Mrs. Torrey,

I am writing this letter on behalf of all of us, the baby-to-be included. We would consider it such a pleasure to have the two of you here for the birth of our baby and your grandchild. Please plan on staying for as long as possible. Anna really does want her mama and papa to be a part of this blessed time in our lives. She would feel so much more secure if you were here with her, and I would feel better knowing that you would be by her side for moral support.

You know the delivery date. It would probably be advisable to come well in advance of the due date, because you already know how unpredictable your daughter is. She may surprise us and have this baby early.

I wait to hear about your expected date of arrival. I'm sure your cousins will be excited to hear that you are arriving early.

Yours truly,

A. G. Kelly

Anna read the invitation and smiled at her husband. "Thank you, A. G. It's a beautiful and sincere letter."

George and Flora arrived the second week of March. John and Neill insisted on picking them up at the depot. They didn't want to take a chance on Anna going into early labor and A. G. not being there.

"Well, well, gonna be a grandpaw, are you?" Neill patted his cousin on the back.

"Finally," George replied. "It's sure been a long time coming."

John joined the conversation. "Flora, you ready to be called Grandma?"

"I don't care what the child calls me. I can hardly wait to get my hands on that baby!"

"Have you had any word from the boys?" George asked.

Neill grunted. "You mean from the prospectors?"

"Yes, are they rich yet?"

"Well, if you call living in a tent in the hills rich, then I guess they are. We were worried about the Indians lifting their scalps, but now we're worried about them starving to death."

Two days later, Elizabeth arrived and put her things in the nursery.

George and Flora decided to stay with the Torreys. Since the boys were gone, there was plenty of room there, but Elizabeth wanted to be closer to the action.

"I won't sleep in that cute little cradle; you can spread me a pallet on the floor. I have to be here for the birth. I know all about that. If you don't believe me, just ask Anna."

"A. G., when I tell you it's time, hurry for Mrs. Crary, because if you leave me here with my sister to take over, we will be in big trouble."

Elizabeth and Anna enjoyed their time together so much that A. G. had to remind them to go to bed, because Anna needed her rest.

"Anna, can you believe we have reached this point in our lives? Here you are, about to have a baby, and here I am, an old maid school teacher." Anna and Elizabeth were in the kitchen, continuing their conversation from the night before.

"Oh, Elizabeth, you aren't old enough to call yourself an old maid."

"What would you call me, Anna?"

"At least a young maid." They both laughed as Elizabeth swung a dish towel at her sister.

"What's for supper, dear sister?" Elizabeth was hoping for a meal at Mrs. Kelly's house to avoid any stomach discomfort.

"I'm making hoe cakes, Elizabeth."

"What? Oh, heaven protect us. I hope Mrs. Kelly is coming over to make them."

"You just wait, Miss Smarty Pants. I've become a pretty good cook since I've been here. You can just ask A. G."

"Will wonders never cease? I'll just do one of those wait-and-see things, if you don't mind."

That night, Mrs. Kelly came over to visit for a while before they retired for the night. She looked out the kitchen window and pointed out the bright full moon in the sky.

"You know what they say about the full moon and babies, don't you?" she asked. "They say it's an old wives' tale that babies are more likely to be born during the full moon if they are due any time close."

"Well, that ol' moon couldn't get any bigger or fuller," Elizabeth said as she looked into the sky full of stars and a moon so bright that it illumined the yard and surrounding foliage. Then, as if on cue, Anna's eyes widened.

"Elizabeth, someone needs to go for Mama and Papa and the midwife. I think it's time for this baby to come."

Mary Kelly called for A. G., who was doing last-minute chores in the barn.

"Is it time?" He was excited and scared at the same time. Looking at Anna and then not waiting for an answer, he ran from the house to the barn, where he hitched the horse to the buggy and made his way at top speed toward Mrs. Crary's house.

"I hope he doesn't scare her to death on the ride back," said Anna with her usual smile.

David Michael ran to the Torreys', which was only a short mile on the little path that they had made through the woods with the back-and-forth visits over the years.

Soon everyone was there. Flora put the coffee pot on the stove in preparation for a long night while Mary Kelly gathered towels and tiny receiving blankets. Mrs. Crary was with Anna, and of course, Elizabeth was there, talking incessantly out of sheer nervousness.

"Elizabeth, you are driving me crazy. Would you slow down? I can't even understand what you are saying. My pains are still very far apart, and you are worse than A. G."

The night wore on, and the contractions were harder and closer together. *I knew there were some reasons why I did not want to get married, and now I know what one of them was,* Elizabeth thought as Anna squeezed her hand with each pain. With Elizabeth at Anna's side, A. G. left the room rather than watch Anna's discomfort with the labor.

It was about one o'clock in the morning when Anna made one final push, and her daughter was born. Elizabeth and A. G. had a bet as to which one would faint first, but both made it through the delivery, although A. G. left the room at one point. The baby girl was welcomed into the world with a chorus of *"Ooooos"* and tears of joy. She was a little baby with a round, angelic face and a head full of black hair pressed into ringlets.

"I think it curls because it's still wet," Anna observed.

"No, Anna, she looks just like you did when you were born." Papa beamed as he looked at his grandchild with the smiling eyes that Anna adored.

"Oh, Papa, isn't she beautiful?"

Papa could only say, "Our little girl." No one knew whether he meant the new baby or Anna.

Taking her sister's hand, Anna said, "Her name is Elizabeth. A. G. and I both agreed that if we had a girl, that was the only name we could give her."

Tears filled Elizabeth's eyes as she looked at her beautiful, tiny namesake.

"If I never have one of my own—if this is as close as I get—it will be enough." And she kissed baby Elizabeth on her soft little cheek.

Chapter 20

Two years later, Anna and A. G.'s second daughter, Flora, was born, and Richard and George returned home with tales of their adventures out west.

"We did encounter Nez Perce." Richard closed his eyes and shook his head from side to side. "They were not warlike people. General Phil Sherman said that we took away their country and means of support and introduced disease and decay to them. This is the reason they made war."

George leaned over the porch rail to spit tobacco juice into the yard. "Chief Joseph surrendered after a seventeen-hundred-mile trip toward Canada. He was hoping to meet up with Sitting Bull there. The soldiers had him convinced they would take the Indians back to their ancestral home."

Michael hung on to every word. "Did they do what they promised?"

George spit again. "Nope, they took them to an Indian reservation where half of them died from disease."

Richard sat on the railing of the porch, one leg swinging to and fro as he talked.

"The Apache tribes were the hardest to hobble. Their chief was called Geronimo, and he hated white men. They were a very prideful people, and I suppose that they would rather die than give over the land that had been theirs for hundreds of years. The killing and mistreatment was far more grave than the slaves."

George agreed that one race was killed in their own country and the other taken from their own country and made into servants.

A. G. wanted to know about the hunting on the plains. "Did you get a chance to hunt any of them big old buffaloes?"

Richard stood up. "The buffalo was the main food source of the Indians, and when the whites came through, they would take their rifles and shoot them from the trains just for sport. There are not too many of them left."

A. G. squinted at Richard. "You sound as though you really feel a kinship to the Indians."

"I'm just disappointed to see the total disregard my race has for others. If I had been on the receiving end of all that treatment, it would cause me to fight. That's the main reason that George and I came home. Up here in these hills, it's like a different world."

Rankin walked out on the porch. "And we are so very glad that you are back."

They all went inside for a meal of fried squirrel and dumplings, greens, fresh tomatoes, and Anna's famous hoe cakes. After lunch, they all went into the living area, where they usually congregated. George and Richard had brought their bags inside and now opened them on the family room floor. Elizabeth sat Indian-style on the floor in front of them, eyes wide with excitement.

"All right, Richard, at the same time, little ones first." They both pulled little brown paper bundles from the bags they held.

Elizabeth untied the string on her gift and also the bow on her little sister's. Both bundles revealed colorful little Indian dolls. They were made of carved wood with painted faces and clothes made of soft buckskin. The hem of the dress was fringed, and a tiny beaded belt completed the doll.

With squeals of delight, Elizabeth jumped to her feet and ran out to better examine her treasure.

Mae called out after her, "Don't play with it outside and get it all dirty."

There was a cradle board for Anna decorated with buckskin ties and colorful paintings of deer on the sides.

"Indian mamas carry their papoose in that thing while they cook their hoe cakes." George grinned as though the comment was his way of complimenting Anna's cooking.

Sarah and Alexandra were the recipients of finely-woven blankets for their beds. The next little package to emerge from the bag was handed to Michael. He could hardly contain his excitement as he began to loosen the string.

"On our way home, we went through Wyoming and Arapaho land, where we picked this up for you, Michael." Richard grinned as he watched Michael's face. The last bit of wrapping fell to the floor to reveal a beautifully crafted, bone-handled knife. Richard stood beside Michael, patting him on the back. "Surely you didn't think we would forget our old tree-climbing buddy."

There were two bright red and yellow clay bowls with paintings of animals in black around the center for Rankin and Mae and small skinning knives for John and Neill.

"We could start our own Indian reservation," John said as he eyed his skinning knife admiringly.

Neill looked at John. "Bet these could really skin a white-tail in a hurry."

There was a gift for everyone; even Mary Kelly got a little Indian basket. Neill turned to his son. "Well, if you did find any gold to speak of, you must have spent it all on these gifts for us."

Richard smiled at his father. "You can buy things from the Indians for just about nothing. Most of the money they get is spent on whiskey."

"That's true, Dad; whiskey is another one of those wonderful gifts that we passed on to them."

The boys were happy to see how pleased everyone was with the gifts they had brought home. The men picked up their chewing tobacco and went out to the porch to talk. The ladies busied themselves with the kitchen and dishes.

"I guess the Indians have had it pretty hard." Mae brushed the crumbs from the table.

"It's really sad. I don't know what I'd do if someone told me I couldn't live here in my house, on my land, because someone else wanted it." Rankin had begun to sweep the floor around the kitchen table.

Mae looked up from her work, deep sadness on her face. "It's the murder of those poor little children that saddens me the most."

The nights were turning much cooler, and the men did not stay on the porch for long after the sun went down. Richard came inside first. "I have really missed these hills and mountains. There are plenty of mountains out west, but there is plenty of desert, rattlesnakes, and horned toads, too."

Michael's ears perked up. "Now I'll bet that's a sight—frogs with horns!"

Richard slapped him on the shoulder. "Yes sir, Michael; you ain't lived till you've seen one. They don't even croak like a frog; they toot like a river boat horn."

"I knew you was lying all the time, Richard. You didn't fool me for a minute. I'm going home and to bed. Maybe I'll see me one of them horned frogs in the woods on the way."

Neill started to walk toward his house. "Come on, Rankin; let's get all these young'uns a place to sleep before I fall out."

"Sarah, you can stay with Alexandra, and that will free up your room for the boys."

Rankin walked toward her house. "I'm sure glad we're so close, or we could really have a big problem."

Neill and the boys were up the next morning just after the sun rose. Neill had just poured a second cup of steaming black coffee and sat down at the table.

"I'm a little worried about Cousin George down in Mississippi. He has been feeling poorly for some time now, but we don't discuss it with Anna, because it upsets her so much."

Rankin walked into the kitchen in her blue gingham work dress, all ready for the new day. "Get that chewing tobacco off my kitchen table, George. You forget how I feel about that?"

"No, ma'am. I got it, and it won't happen again."

Rankin bustled about the kitchen as she began to prepare breakfast. Richard sat up straight so he could possibly see what she was making for breakfast.

"Mama, we having flapjacks?"

"No, eggs and bacon."

"Oh, Mama, I ain't had flapjacks since I left home. They cook something they call waffles, and they're so tough, you can't even cut 'em."

"Well, I'll see if I can whip you up a little stack."

George leaned back in his chair and winked at Richard. "You know what I really miss the most about things out west are them dancing girls in the saloons."

Rankin whirled around to face her sons. "I can't believe my ears!" Mama was off and running.

George looked at his brother with a big grin on his face. "It's so good to be back home," he whispered.

Chapter 21

Elizabeth had just returned to school from her Thanksgiving break. She had gone to Tehvah to see about Flora and George. Her father did not look well, and she was quite worried about his condition. Aunt Lucy had died the year before, and Elizabeth had fallen heir to her home in Clinton. Elizabeth had moved from the dorm room at school and was now comfortably settled into Aunt Lucy's house.

An old maid living in an old maid's house, Elizabeth thought as she settled in at the kitchen table to finish up the grading that needed to be completed before class. Her mind wandered back to the first year she began to teach and all the problems that her students faced. They had come quite a long way with their education, and the school had grown. She thought of the ones who had graduated and gone on to attend college—especially Mary. Tiny Bell had been the talker and Elizabeth thought that surely she would become a lawyer or sell Robertson's Infallible Worm-Destroying Lozenges.

Elizabeth recalled the beaming face of Sunshine Leeds and her struggles with English grammar, especially the verb *be.* She was not ready to do a Shakespearean play at year's end but was well on her way to using good English.

She remembered Ruthie Jackson and all the resentment that she had about her life. Of all the children in her first-year class, Ruthie proved to be the hardest one to reach. She was hard and discontented with life in general and the place in which she found herself. She trusted no one, because she felt that everyone had let her down. This had proven to be Elizabeth's biggest challenge, but after a year of working at it, Elizabeth had broken through, and Ruthie had begun to blossom.

Elizabeth put her grading pencil on the table beside her papers and leaned thoughtfully back in her chair. She reminisced about the Mississippi Rifles—in particular, a very handsome, young, blonde boy. She wondered why she did not go with him when he asked her to let him walk her around the campus at Mississippi College years before.

I guess it was just stupidity, she thought. Shaking her head a little, she came back to reality. She didn't know why she was feeling nostalgic; she was perfectly content with her life as it was. *Yes,* she thought, *I've been truly blessed.* She finished grading her papers and retired for the night, not the least bit melancholy.

The next day, Elizabeth was thrilled to receive a letter from Anna. She got a cup of tea and settled into the big chair in the parlor to enjoy her sister's letter.

> Dear Elizabeth,
>
> Hope you are well and enjoying your teaching duties. I vow I don't know how that could be possible, but it seems to be what you enjoy doing.
>
> You would be so proud of me! I can make hoe cakes almost as good as Izzy. Maybe someday I'll break down and show you how I do it.
>
> Elizabeth and Flora are growing very fast and getting prettier every day. Would you believe it—they have real Indian dolls to play with? If you remember, you and I had dolls from the corn stalks in the garden. George and Richard brought them back from the west and brought me a little

cradle board for Flora. Of course, she is too big for it now, but it's the thought that counts.

I really wanted to know what you know about Papa's health. No one around here will talk with me for long about it. They don't seem to think that I'm too strong or maybe not grown-up enough. Honestly, Elizabeth, I get so frustrated with them sometimes—especially A. G. I really need to know how he is and if something is seriously wrong.

Do you have a beau yet, or do you still plan on living a life of solitude?

I seem to be rambling on and on when what I really want to know is any news that you may have about Papa.

Please, Elizabeth, tell me about Papa …

Your sister,

Anna

Placing the letter on the small table beside her tea, Elizabeth sighed, closed her eyes, and cupped her forehead in her hands. *I don't know, Anna,* she thought. *I just don't know.*

The next day, Elizabeth dismissed her class when Sarah Dickey walked through the door. Elizabeth looked up. "Am I being dismissed? This is quite a surprise to have you visit my classroom."

Miss Dickey stood in the door until Elizabeth invited her into the room. She wore her usual high-collar blouse, much like the one that Elizabeth was wearing, and a long black skirt. Her dark hair was pulled back in a most severe fashion and fastened low on the back of her neck. *How stern she looks,* Elizabeth thought as she remembered how compassionate the lady really was.

Sarah moved forward toward Elizabeth. "I would like to talk with you for just a moment, if you have the time."

"Of course. Take this chair by my desk."

"Elizabeth, we have a wealthy contributor to our school who needs help with his daughter and her schooling. In short, she needs an English tutor. I have taken it upon myself to set up an appointment for him to talk with you tomorrow after school. I know I should have consulted you beforehand, but he is such a busy man—and most of all, he is a most generous contributor to our school. I really hope you will consider this an opportunity to increase your income as well."

Elizabeth showed some surprise at Sarah's initiative. "Of course. I'll be happy to discuss it with him."

"His name is Raymond McIntire, and I have asked him to be here in your classroom by three o'clock. Elizabeth, please give it every consideration."

"I will."

The next afternoon, Elizabeth waited at her desk for her visitor. She had dismissed her class a few minutes early to give herself time to collect her thoughts on why she could not offer Mr. McIntire's little daughter any time for tutoring. She did have time in the afternoon for such a class, and for that reason, she felt a bit guilty as she heard the quiet knock at her open door. She looked up to see a tall, middle-aged man standing in the door. His fashionable stove pipe hat in hand, he waited to be invited inside. Elizabeth fumbled nervously with the cameo brooch at her throat, feeling uncomfortable.

"Do come in, Mr. McIntire."

Taking her extended hand, he looked into her eyes and smiled. "It's a pleasure to meet you, Miss Torrey. Miss Dickey has told me so many good things about you."

"Please have a seat, Mr. McIntire." She motioned to the chair near her desk. His black frock coat and grey pin-striped trousers gave him the look of a very successful man. A gold watch chain was draped across his vest.

"Miss Torrey, I don't know what Miss Dickey has told you about my dilemma, but I have a very precious little seven-year-old who is struggling with her schoolwork. She has been having problems since her mother's death. She is all I have now, and I only want to make life a little easier for her, if that is possible."

Elizabeth looked into the man's clear blue eyes and wondered why she had not met him earlier. "How many days a week were you expecting for her tutoring?"

"As many as you can give her, Miss Torrey."

"Please call me Elizabeth." Why had she said that? She felt that perhaps she had been too bold. Her mind was soon put to rest with his tactful reply.

"Thank you, Elizabeth; that will make it easier for me. To tell the truth, I wasn't sure how to pronounce your last name."

"We can begin your daughter's lessons next week, if that will be agreeable to you."

Standing up to leave, he smiled at Elizabeth. "The sooner the better—and I would consider it a favor if you would address me as Raymond."

As he left the room, Elizabeth realized that she had not even asked the child's name. "I would like to know your daughter's name."

"Of course—forgive me. Her name is Annabel." He smiled and was gone.

Elizabeth sat down again at her desk. Had she just met the most perfect man in the world besides Papa? She suddenly could not wait to tell Anna—but what was there to tell? Maybe she would give this a little more time.

The first of the week finally came, and Elizabeth found herself waiting excitedly for Raymond and Annabel to arrive at her classroom. At the appointed time, they arrived. Raymond did not wear his frock coat or hat this time but still looked quite dapper in dark blue trousers, a white shirt, and a vest. Annabel was a tiny little thing with round cheeks, much like Elizabeth had remembered Anna at that age.

"Good afternoon, Elizabeth. This is my Annabel."

The little girl curtsied as she held her little pink dress at both sides.

"My goodness, such fine manners you have, Annabel."

"My mama taught me to curtsy." Annabel smiled at Elizabeth's approval.

"Are you ready to get started with some fun learning?"

"Oh, yes, please."

Elizabeth told Raymond good-bye, showed Annabel a desk that she could use, and sat down in the desk beside her to get better acquainted with her.

"Tell me, Annabel, do you have any pets at home or favorite dolls you like to play with?"

As the weeks passed, Elizabeth and Annabel got to be quite good friends, and Elizabeth became more at ease around Raymond. He was such a gentleman that Elizabeth found it difficult to believe that she was on the receiving end of such respect.

At the end of one of the sessions, when Raymond came by to collect Annabel, he quietly asked Elizabeth if she might enjoy going to dinner with him on the weekend. Elizabeth was very flattered and tried not to appear too eager with her acceptance.

"Can you believe it?" Elizabeth wrote in her letter to Anna.

I am not saying that anything will come of this new acquaintance, but I can't remember being so happy. He may just be looking for a companion for Annabel, and that would be understandable, but I find myself hoping for more. That's the extent of my good news.

As far as Papa's condition, Anna, I really don't know what to tell you. It's not because I think you wouldn't know how to handle it but simply that I don't know. You and I may need to pay Mama and Papa a visit for a few days and see what we think for ourselves. Write and let me know how you feel about that. I know that you have Elizabeth and Flora to consider—and A. G., of course.

Till I hear from you again, I miss you and love you very much.

Elizabeth

At the end of the week, Elizabeth finished her session with Annabel and waited for Raymond to pick up his daughter. Elizabeth hoped that he had not forgotten their dinner date, because it had not been mentioned again since that time.

With a light tap at the classroom door, Raymond appeared with his usual pleasant smile. "You ready to go, princess?" Annabel ran to meet her father and jumped into his arms.

"Miss Elizabeth, would five o'clock tomorrow night meet with your approval for dinner? I thought we might drive to Vicksburg and try a new restaurant called Creole. I've heard their New Orleans–style food is very tasty."

"Sounds wonderful. I will be ready. I live on Main Street in downtown Clinton."

"Yes, I know," he said with a smile.

Why did I do that? she thought. *Now he thinks that I'm scared to death he can't find my house! I suppose he is figuring on driving time to Vicksburg being an hour or so. That means after we order, get our food, and drive home it would be close to nine o'clock when I get home. Well, I don't care if the neighbors think I am a floozy.* She picked up her papers to be graded and started her short walk home from school, humming softly to herself.

Most of Saturday morning was spent in trying to decide which dress to wear and how to fix her hair. Elizabeth finally decided on a lilac skirt and lacy white blouse with a high neck, puff sleeves, and a white bow at the yoke. Her tiny waist was emphasized by the wide band on the skirt.

The dinner was perfect, but the moonlight ride home was far more wonderful. Elizabeth could not deny the feelings that she had for Raymond and wondered if his feelings were as strong as hers. As they pulled the carriage up to Elizabeth's house that night, Raymond took her hand to help her down.

"I had a wonderful time tonight, Raymond."

"We will just have to do it again." He took her hand, and bowing his head slightly with his eyes still on hers, kissed her hand softly. "As you may have guessed, I have grown quite fond of you, Elizabeth." He paused as though waiting for a response from his companion. He continued, "I would like for you to see Rosewood. If you like, I'll have our cook fix you a nice home-cooked meal next week."

"I never turn down an invitation for a home-cooked meal." *What a stupid reply to that invitation. I sound like I go around eating all the time.* Elizabeth's thoughts on how she sounded always bothered her.

Raymond held her hand as they walked to the door, and Elizabeth felt like she knew how Anna must have felt that day at the station when A. G. swept her up in his arms.

"Good night. Thank you for a wonderful night."

Elizabeth felt that her feet never even touched the ground as she floated inside.

I do declare, I feel just like a little ol' butterfly. Once again, she was mocking Anna's saccharine sweet Southern belle drawl, but she meant every word.

Chapter 22

Anna opened Elizabeth's letter and sat down with a plop. "A. G., get me a glass of water, because I feel like I'm going to faint!"

"What's wrong, Anna?"

"Elizabeth is in love. I can't believe it."

"With who?"

"He's some rich planter who lives near Clinton. Elizabeth is tutoring his little girl. Seems like his wife died of a fever a couple of years ago. She has been out with him only a couple of times."

"Sometimes that's all it takes."

"She says he's such a gentleman. Maybe I ought to send you up there to get a few lessons, A. G."

Anna read on. "She says that she doesn't know anything about Papa's condition, but maybe she and I could take a trip to Tehvah and check on him ourselves."

"That may be a good idea just to set your mind at ease. We have enough folks here that we could take care of the girls." Elizabeth came in when she heard her mama talking about going to Tehvah.

"Mama, you going to see Grandma and Grandpa?"

"I don't know yet, sweetheart. Aunt Elizabeth and I are talking about it. Is that all right with you if we go?"

"Can I go, Mama? I like visiting them too."

"Well, not this time, but we will plan a trip when you and Flora can go with us. A. G., when do you think we could go?"

"I don't know, Anna. Maybe you had better let Elizabeth decide, since she will have to plan around school—and now with her new beau."

In Clinton, Elizabeth was trying to deal with Raymond's request to meet her family at Tehvah. She had thought of taking him when she and Anna made the trip home to check on Papa's health but wasn't sure how that would work. It could be a little bit too much for Papa. She would give it some thought before she answered Anna's letter.

Raymond and Elizabeth had discussed marriage, but she knew that Raymond wanted to talk with Papa and ask him for her hand. For this reason, Elizabeth had decided to make a trip to Tehvah with Raymond in advance of her trip with Anna.

School was out for the summer, and Elizabeth thought this would be a good time to introduce Raymond to her parents. Raymond made sure that business at Rosewood would go on for a day or two while they were away, and they made the short trip to Tehvah. Zeb met them in the drive and took care of the bags and the horse. Inside, Elizabeth was met by Flora and ushered into the west room, where Papa was sitting in his big chair beneath the great window, reading glasses on his nose and a book in his hand. Elizabeth ran to him and threw her arms around his neck. Kissing him on the cheek, she stepped back and took Raymond's hand in hers.

"Mama, Papa, this is Raymond McIntire. He has been anxious to meet you." Turning and looking lovingly into Raymond's eyes, she continued, "I will leave you in my papa's capable hands. I want to talk to Mama for just a minute."

As Elizabeth and Mama turned to walk from the room, Elizabeth's eyes fell on the light shawl that Papa had across his lap, even though the weather was warm and sunny.

Elizabeth was concerned. "Mama, Papa looks so tired. Has Dr. Buie seen him lately?"

"You know your father." Flora fidgeted with her apron. "He doesn't like to cause a stir and says that there is nothing wrong with his health."

"Anna wants to come home and check on him. I told her that we could plan a trip together if you don't think it would be too much for the two of you."

"That might be just the medicine your father needs. He does miss the two of you so much."

Elizabeth told her mother of their plans for a wedding. "We just want a very small ceremony at the parsonage. Raymond's first wife died two years ago, and he has the most adorable little girl named Annabel." Elizabeth took her mother's hand, "Mama, I just love him so much. I know he is the one God chose for me."

"Well, let's go and see how well Raymond is doing with your father." Flora wiped the corners of her eyes with the bottom of her apron and followed Elizabeth back down the hall to the west room.

"How are things going here?" Elizabeth tried not to sound nervous.

"He hasn't thrown me out yet," answered Raymond, "And I suppose that's a good sign."

Papa took off his glasses and placed them on the table beside the chair. "He seems like a nice enough fellow. I just hope he will still have that calmness and cheerful attitude when the two of you have been married for a few years."

Elizabeth ran to her father and knelt beside him. "Thank you, Papa, but I knew you would like him. After all, he is a lot like you."

The visit went well. Elizabeth showed Raymond around Tehvah and all the places that she and Anna enjoyed. He seemed to want to know all he could about Elizabeth and how she was as a child. They walked to the creek and back to the garden, where Raymond looked at the field and the twelve little cottages.

"Sometimes I wish that Rosewood was a little smaller. It would be much easier to manage, and I would have more time to spend with you and Annabel."

The sun was warm, and a slight breeze blew as they walked back in the direction of the little family cemetery. He held Elizabeth's hand and smiled down at her.

"You have some fond memories of Tehvah and your childhood here, don't you?"

"I really do, and it's hard to believe that so much time has passed. I suppose the old saying about time waiting for no man is true. At any point in time, you can always scratch your head and ask the question, 'Where has the time gone?'"

The cemetery was pretty this time of year. Forsythia and spider lilies bloomed around the black wrought iron fence. Raymond looked at the smaller tombstones. "Who are the children buried here, Elizabeth?"

Elizabeth told him about her little brother, Hugh, and then about her father's twin brothers. They walked to the back porch steps in silence and sat at the bottom stoop for a moment before either one of them spoke.

"We have both had our share of tragedies in our lives, but right now, we are happy, and that's what we must remember. We will probably have other moments of sadness, but together, we can come out on the other side."

"I suppose so." Elizabeth smiled at him. "Other people do it all the time." Raymond took Elizabeth by the hand and helped her to her feet.

The next morning, Raymond and Elizabeth left for Clinton, still not knowing what to tell Anna about Papa. He seemed to be fine when the family was around him but looked tired and pale.

"What did Papa tell you when you asked him about us getting married?"

"He told me to get lost."

"No, really, what did he say?"

"Well, first he asked me if I had the ability to support you properly, and next he asked me if I loved you enough to die for you. I thought that was a strange thing to ask me, but I told him yes and yes."

"You would have to know my Papa to understand the last question."

"No, I have Annabel, and I know exactly why he asked that question."

Elizabeth slipped closer to Raymond and slipped her arm around his. "I'm just the luckiest woman on the face of the earth."

"What did you say, dear? I didn't hear you."

"Oh, nothing. I was just thinking out loud."

The horse clopped along at a slow, steady pace. The day was young, and the two passengers were in no particular hurry to get home. It seemed that all nature was cooperating with Elizabeth and Raymond that day. The leaves rustled in the gentle breeze, and the birds lent their voices to the quiet peace that surrounded them.

"Do you feel the contentment that I feel?"

"Yes, my dear, I do."

"I wish we could always feel this way."

The drive from Tehvah ended all too soon for Elizabeth and Raymond, but Raymond had his duties back at Rosewood, and Elizabeth had to write a long letter to Anna about her short visit home.

Elizabeth went in to unpack and hang her clothes. For the first time, as she entered the parlor, Elizabeth noticed the smell of lilac talcum powder. Was that her imagination, or had Anna been right all along about how Aunt Lucy's house smelled? She would have to consider selling Aunt Lucy's house after she and Raymond were married.

Elizabeth put on her comfortable slippers and sat down at her writing desk.

Dear Anna,

This letter will be a short one. I am a little tired from my trip to Tehvah. Raymond wanted to talk to Papa about marrying his little girl. Yes, we have decided to take the big step. If we were having a big wedding, you would surely be my maid of honor, but we have decided on a very small wedding at the parsonage. As you already know, Raymond's first wife died, and I don't want Annabel to think that I'm trying to replace her mother.

I had a chance to talk with Papa, and although he looks a little pale and tired, I think his health is generally good. If you like, we can still make a trip home. Just let me know when you want to go, and if it doesn't interfere with my wedding, we will go.

Give my love to Elizabeth and Flora and A. G.

Your wonderful sister,

Elizabeth Torrey (McIntire)

How childish you are, Elizabeth, she thought. *You sound just like a lovesick little girl.*

Chapter 23

The wedding was small, as promised. Elizabeth beamed as she stood with Raymond before Reverend Gage, the pastor of the little Presbyterian church in Clinton. Anna and A. G. made the trip from Arkansas, and to Elizabeth's great delight, she had her maid of honor. Zeb drove Mama and Papa to Clinton for the wedding. Anna stood beside Elizabeth along with Annabel, who seemed to be very happy with the union.

Elizabeth was beautiful in Flora's wedding dress. She was afraid that it would not fit around her waist, but it fit like it was made for her. Flora had protected it as well as she could, hoping that one day, one of her children could wear it on her special day. The lace was not as pristine as it once had been, but the satin of the gown still fell in soft folds to the floor. The high neck was fastened with a tasteful diamond brooch that was given to Elizabeth by Raymond.

When the "I do's" were said, the couple changed into their travel clothes and were driven to the train station for their trip to New Orleans. From there, they were taking a trip to Europe.

A. G. looked at Anna's smiling face. "We should have taken a trip after our wedding."

"We did, A. G. We went to Arkansas."

"That's not going to Europe and seeing all the sights we have never seen before." A. G. felt a little jealous of Raymond's wealth and ability to give Elizabeth things that he could not give to Anna.

"A. G., you showed me some of the most beautiful scenery in the world. There are clear, blue lakes and the most beautiful mountains on God's green earth, and we don't have to leave to go home." Anna took his hand in hers. "We are home."

Mama and Papa were driven to Rosewood in the carriage with Annabel. They were invited to stay there for as long as they wished.

The carriage pulled up to the steps of Rosewood. It was a huge working plantation home twice as big as Tehvah. There were four large columns with an ionic capital set atop each shaft. A column on each end of the front helped support the balcony that ran the entire length of the house. Ornate cast iron rails covered the open spaces between the columns. The Magnolia trees on the front lawn were large and in full bloom.

"Oh," Flora said as she sniffed the air, "the smell of all those blossoms is breathtaking."

Annabel jumped from the carriage and ran toward the steps. The carriage driver retrieved their bag and helped Flora from the carriage. They were greeted at the door by the housekeeper, Delilah. Strangely enough, she reminded Flora of Izzy.

"Do come on in, and welcome to Rosewood. I fixed your room, and you can fix for dinner. I show you the room." They followed her up the winding stair case to the large room on the second floor. Delilah opened the door for them to reveal a massive oak bed and round oak table in the center of the room with a bowl of fresh magnolia blossoms. The fireplace had a mantle of oak with intricate carvings of leaves and acorns.

"Well." Papa took in Flora's reaction to the elaborate sight. "I guess you won't even want to go back home."

"You know, George, what I was really thinking was how I would hate to keep all this stuff dusted and clean."

Quite pleased with Flora's answer to his probing comment, he reached for her hand and smiled.

The next day, Annabel was anxious to show Flora and George the rest of the grounds. Elizabeth had told her that they were to be her new grandparents, and she was very excited to meet them.

George had decided to stay in the room and do a little reading, but Flora was anxious to tour the grounds. She followed Annabel down the stairs and out the heavy front door.

"Let's go to the back, and I'll show you my swing and playhouse." Taking Flora's hand, she skipped around the side of the house with her new grandma in tow.

Annabel was headed for a little white playhouse in the middle of the yard, but Flora gazed at seemingly endless rows of cotton. The rows stretched all the way to the distant tree line of the woods, which could have been half a mile away.

Annabel pulled Flora toward her playhouse. Above the front door was a squinch—placed there, Flora thought, to give it the same look of elegance as the plantation itself. It was like a fairy tale.

"Daddy had this built for me after Mama died. Do you like it, Grandma?"

"It's just beautiful, Annabel. I almost expect to see King Arthur and the Knights of the Round Table inside your castle."

"Really?"

"Sure. You know, when we pretend, we can see lots of things." Flora stooped down a little to go inside the house. "What do you hope to see when you go inside, Annabel?"

"I had really hoped to see my mother, but I never did."

Flora took Annabel's hand. Trying to change the subject, she asked about the porcelain doll lying on the tiny bed in the corner.

A. G. and Anna decided to stay at Aunt Lucy's house instead of Rosewood even though Anna did not look forward to the smell of the parlor. She thought that Elizabeth may have come up with something to rectify that problem. They walked inside the modest little home.

"Nope, it's still here."

"What's still here, Anna?"

"Don't you smell it? That old folks' talcum smell!"

"Well, I never. You're just imagining that, Anna. It doesn't smell any different than any other house."

She kicked off her walking shoes. "I guess I just have a sensitive nose."

A. G. and Anna took a stroll through Clinton on their first day after the wedding and looked at the antebellum homes that still remained after the burning during the Civil War. Anna wanted to visit Rosewood but did not want A. G. to feel that he had not provided for her as well as Raymond had for her sister.

The honeymooners arrived in Scotland. Elizabeth knew that her ancestors had come from the area of Campbelltown and the Isle of Skye. She had heard her great-grandma talk about the beauty of the land, the red deer, and the shaggy cattle. She wanted to see the blooming heather as well as the castle in Edinburgh.

She had also hoped to visit Armadale Castle, which was built in 1790, but learned that it was destroyed by fire a few years earlier in 1855.

There was still much to see in this country that felt like home to Elizabeth. Her mother's ancestors were a sept of the clan MacDonald, and Elizabeth remembered the story told by her mother of the Clan Donald's important part in religious and political affairs in Scotland. Donald became the founder of the Clan Donald, which literally meant the "children of Donald" giving his descendants the name MacDonald, or "son of Donald."

"Raymond, this is such a wonderful place. I hope that one day I can bring Mama and Papa here to see it. You know, we have all heard stories about it for years, but you never get the full impact until you are standing on the very spot where the history began."

"We will plan another trip for the family soon. Right now, I think you need to sample the local cuisine."

"And just what, pray tell, would that be?"

"Why, haggis, my dear."

"No, Raymond. No!"

Chapter 24

Raymond and Elizabeth arrived back at Rosewood after spending a month in Europe. Mama and Papa were back at Tehvah, and Anna and A. G. were in their cozy little home in Arkansas. Presents were unpacked from the trunk for Annabel, and she was given her gifts before Delilah came into the room. Annabel's favorite gift was a miniature bagpipe that sounded like two angry cats fighting.

"We might need to find someone to give you a few lessons," Raymond said with a laugh. Annabel hurried downstairs, still squeezing the bagpipe and marching as she went. "What were you thinking, Elizabeth? I will remember that this was your idea."

Elizabeth took Delilah's gift from the trunk and placed it on the bed.

"I need to tell you a little bit about Delilah. She has been the housekeeper and lady of the manor, so to speak, for two years now and will be suspicious of your intentions. So don't be too surprised if you are not made very welcome at first."

Elizabeth kissed her husband on the cheek. "I understand completely. I am not completely without understanding."

Delilah entered with a pot of hot tea and a plate of tea cakes. "Hello, Delilah." Elizabeth smiled as she took the tray. "I'm so glad you came up, and thank you for bringing the tea. It's just what we needed. We did bring you a little gift back from Scotland."

Delilah eyed Elizabeth suspiciously as she produced the little hat box from the bed. Handing it to Delilah, she smiled. "This is for you."

Delilah took the box, untied the ribbon on the top, and looked inside. Delilah gave a little gasp as she removed the delicate blue bonnet inside.

"I ain't never had me somethin' so nice before." She wiped her eyes on her apron and quickly left the room.

"I think you just made a new friend, dear. Delilah has always been a little short on words, especially when it comes to expressing her gratitude. She was very close to Annabel's mother, but I think you have won her over."

The next few days were spent getting acquainted with Rosewood and the daily routine of Annabel and Raymond. Sometimes Elizabeth went to the fields with Raymond when he made his rounds. Other times she spent with Annabel, working on her schooling—but most of all, she stayed out of Delilah's way. She did not want Delilah to perceive her as a threat. She stayed in touch with Anna and wrote Mama and Papa a long letter about the places she visited and things she saw in Scotland. She mentioned the possibility of taking a family trip back there in the near future.

Elizabeth tried to spend a good amount of time each day with Annabel—not because she felt it was a part of her job as Annabel's stepmother but because she genuinely enjoyed being around her. Elizabeth went down the hall to Annabel's room toward the screeching sound of the bagpipe. Uncovering her ears as she entered the room, Elizabeth stepped in front of Annabel to alert her of her presence in the room and end the practice.

Annabel put down her instrument on the bed. "Hello, Elizabeth." She was her usual cheerful self and smiled up at Elizabeth.

"Hello. I thought that I would just pop in for a spot of tea—that is, if you think the Queen will be in attendance."

Annabel's eyes danced with excitement. "Oh, I'm quite sure she will arrive at any minute." Annabel ran to the little cupboard and retrieved the porcelain teapot and three cups that Elizabeth brought her from Europe. They sat on the floor, and Annabel poured imaginary tea for both of them.

Elizabeth sipped her tea and carried on polite conversation. "Will you be in attendance at the ball tomorrow night, Princess?"

"Oh, yes, I have a lovely blue ballgown and some glass slippers."

"I should like to try on that gown."

"Oh, no, you are much too fat!"

Elizabeth had played this game many times, but this was a new twist. "My, my, if you were not the Princess, I would be most offended by that remark."

"Oh, Mother, you know that I was only playing a game."

Elizabeth was silent for a moment. She could not believe that Annabel had just called her *Mother.*

Delilah came into the room to announce that dinner would be ready shortly and that Annabel should wash her hands. Elizabeth had gotten past all the awkward moments with Delilah and felt that she had at last gained Delilah's confidence and trust.

Raymond was at home, and the whole family sat down at the long dining room table. Unlike Tehvah, the food was served bowl by bowl so each diner could take what he or she wanted.

"I thought that in a few weeks, we might have a dinner party so that our neighbors could meet you and see what a fortunate man I am."

"Raymond, I'm not the most gifted hostess in the world. You will have to give me some pointers so that I won't be an embarrassment to you."

"I'm sure that you will be the most elegant, gracious hostess anywhere."

"Yes, Father, we have tea with the Queen!"

The weeks went by quickly, and Elizabeth settled into her routine more easily than first imagined. Raymond had talked with her about the possibility of giving up her job at the school in order to spend more time with him and Annabel. She loved her job but thought Raymond was right, since she had become a wife and mother all at once. She had felt a bit tired and sick for the past month. Raymond insisted on her seeing the doctor.

Elizabeth was concerned. Papa had been sick, and now she was sick. She thought of all the things that needed to be done as she climbed the stairs to Dr. Patterson's office.

What would Raymond do if I got too sick to get around and take care of Rosewood and Annabel? She said a little prayer as she opened the door to Dr. Patterson's office.

A kindly face greeted her. The doctor was a portly man of about sixty-five with a bald spot on his head that reminded Elizabeth of a monk. He wore wire-framed glasses and looked at her over the top of them—much like Papa did when he waited for her to tell him about a problem. She was instantly at ease in his office. After the examination, he sat down with Elizabeth.

"What is wrong with me? I hope I'm not dying." Elizabeth laughed nervously at her crude attempt at humor.

Dr. Patterson smiled at her. "No, my dear, nothing quite so grave as that. Had the thought ever occurred to you that you may be pregnant?"

Elizabeth dropped her purse on the floor. Being ever the southern gentleman, the good doctor stooped to retrieve it at the same time as Elizabeth.

"Are you all right?" Elizabeth gave him a nasty head-butt.

"I don't think it will require hospitalization," he replied, rubbing his head.

All the way on her buggy ride back to Rosewood, Elizabeth tried to imagine the best way to tell Raymond the good news. They never mentioned another child, and suddenly a chill came over her. Maybe Raymond did not want other children. Perhaps he felt Annabel was the only one he wanted in his life. She shook her head as she drove up to the steps of Rosewood. That would not be possible.

Raymond was at home, waiting to hear about Elizabeth's visit to the doctor. Elizabeth had asked that he not go with her, and he had respected her wishes.

"Tell me what the doctor said. I've been waiting

Annabel walked in the room. "Well, he said that he felt that I should quit my job and take life easy."

"And why is that?" Raymond was becoming frustrated.

"Annabel, get your tea set, and let's have tea with the Queen."

Raymond could not believe his ears. "Elizabeth, I want you to tell me what the doctor said."

Annabel had set her tea set on the floor. "Well, if you want to know all the details, you will have to have a cup of tea with us."

Raymond plopped down on the floor and realized that Elizabeth wanted to include Annabel in this conversation. Annabel poured tea, and they began their ritual of having tea with the Queen.

"For heaven's sake, Elizabeth, what did the doctor say?"

"He said that this time next year, we will have to have another teacup. Annabel is going to get another playmate, and you won't have to curl your long legs up on the floor to entertain anyone."

Raymond was in shock. "When, Elizabeth?"

"About seven months."

Raymond jumped to his feet and gently helped Elizabeth to her feet so he could embrace her.

"Is our tea party over? The Queen isn't even here yet." Annabel's face registered displeasure.

"Annabel, you are going to have a little brother or sister to play with soon." Raymond looked at Annabel with tears in his eyes and a broad grin. "I'm going to tell Delilah." Raymond raced from the room toward the kitchen.

That evening, Delilah prepared a feast to celebrate the news. "We's got ham, sweet taters, collard greens, 'maters, corn pone, and pumpkin pie."

"That sounds wonderful," Elizabeth said as she sat down and waited for the serving to commence.

"You eatin' for two now, Miss Lizabeth. I be makin' sure you gets lots of good food to eat."

"I know you will, Delilah. I know I can count on you." Elizabeth could not remember when she had been this happy—maybe never.

Elizabeth wanted to tell Anna in person, but realizing that would not be possible, sat down the next morning to write her about her good news.

> Dear Anna,
>
> Just a short note to say hello and let you know that we are all doing well here. Hope Elizabeth and Flora are well.
>
> I went to the doctor the other day, because I had been feeling rather tired and run down. He assured me that everything was all right and that I was not about to die.
>
> The cotton crop looks great, but it requires a great deal of Raymond's time away from me.
>
> I do want you, A. G., and the children to come for a visit before long. Annabel would love playing tea party with her cousins. Tell all the cousins that we send our love. Write and let me hear from you soon.
>
> Love,
>
> Your sister, Elizabeth
>
> Oh, yes, I'm pregnant.

Elizabeth smiled as she sealed Anna's letter. She took out another sheet of paper.

> Dear Mama and Papa,
>
> I hope that the two of you are well. Please tell Simmy that I'm counting on her to take care of both of you.

I have some news that I think you might find exciting.

I'm going to have a baby! That is a surprise coming from one who never even expected to get married at all. I hope that you can be here when the baby is born. You know I really don't know too much about babies being born—just ask Anna.

If the baby is a boy, there is only one name that we have even considered, and I'm sure you know that it will be George Torrey McIntire.

Elizabeth was in her fourth month when she felt the movement of the baby. There was no doubt that there was life within her, and she could hardly wait for Raymond to feel the little flutters.

In the fifth month of her pregnancy, Elizabeth sat down very carefully on the floor for Annabel's tea party with the Queen. "Mother." Annabel looked up, and her eyes came to rest on Elizabeth's stomach. "I hope you can have more tea parties with me."

"Of course I will, darling. Why do you say that?"

"Because you are really fat, and I'm afraid that you won't be able to sit on the floor if you get much fatter."

"Well, if I do, I'll just have to sit in a chair, won't I?"

Annabel, satisfied with Elizabeth's answer, smiled and poured another cup of tea.

Elizabeth could not magine her life being any happier. Raymond loved her and was a very attentive husband, Annabel loved her and called her Mother, and Delilah had accepted her as the lady of the house. Papa seemed to be improving, and the crops were doing very well—and of course, she was carrying a baby. Elizabeth thought that this was the point in time where she could say, "And they lived happily ever after."

But that was not to be.

Chapter 25

It was a cold morning at Rosewood. It was probably the last cold day of the year, and everyone looked forward to an early spring, as tiny buds began to appear on the trees. The McIntires were gathered around the dining table for a late brunch. The cool morning had brought the temptation to sleep in. Elizabeth went to the door, because Delilah was still in the kitchen, humming happily.

Elizabeth came back to the table and opened the telegram she had just received. "My dear Elizabeth. We need you at home ..."

In Arkansas, it was still snowing slightly, but the cold was not as severe as it had been. A. G. came into the little house with a telegram for Anna. She opened the identical telegram that Elizabeth had received.

"My dear Anna, we need you at home. Papa has passed away. Mama." She dropped the telegram, and a sick feeling swept over her. "A. G., my papa is dead. What do I do now?" She began to weep uncontrollably. Papa would know what to do, but he was gone. Anna was a little girl once more and missed her papa's comfort in her sorrow.

A. G. did what he could to comfort Anna but could find no solace for her pain. Mary Kelly came in, and A. G. told her the news. "Let me try, A. G., and you explain what is going on to the girls. Someone will have to break the news to John and Neill as well."

Mary went into the bedroom, where Anna lay across the bed, sobbing. "I know your heart is broken, dear, but you must also consider the living.

Your mother needs you now, and your children don't understand all your sadness." As Mary's words began to sink in, Anna quieted her sobs, and Mary left the room.

A. G. asked his mother if she would be willing to break the news to the cousins. As Mary walked down the path to John's house, she wondered if the news might hit the cousins almost as hard as it had Anna.

Back at Rosewood, Elizabeth finished the telegram and fainted, her head striking the table. Raymond rushed to her side. "Elizabeth, Elizabeth, are you all right?" He patted her hand, dipped a napkin into the water glass, and wiped her forehead. Elizabeth opened her eyes and stared at Raymond blankly. "Are you all right, Elizabeth?"

Elizabeth picked up the telegram on her plate and handed it to him. "Oh my dear, I am so very sorry. Delilah, would you please take Annabel upstairs with maybe a little real tea for her tea pot?" Annabel knew that something was wrong but was obedient and went with Delilah to the kitchen for tea and toast.

"Oh, Raymond, I can't believe that Papa is gone. It was an extra blessing that we got to visit Papa before he got too sick to enjoy our visit. I know that Anna is beyond comfort. A. G. is a good husband to Anna, but he isn't Papa. We need to go as soon as possible, Raymond. Mama needs us there, I'm sure. I think it best if Annabel is not exposed to this kind of sadness again. Maybe she should stay at Rosewood with Delilah."

"Do you feel up to the trip?"

"It's not that far, and I have had no problems. Mama will need me—and Anna as well."

The next morning, the carriage left Rosewood on its short trip to Tehvah and the last visit to see Papa. In Arkansas, A. G., Anna, and the girls were driven to the depot to catch the train for Mississippi and the last visit with Papa. A. G. dreaded the long trip. He could not fill in for Papa.

Elizabeth and Raymond were the first to arrive at Tehvah. After Raymond helped Elizabeth down from the carriage, he took the horse to the barn. Zeb was usually there to help, but Zeb was in mourning for George, just as the rest of the Tehvah family. Elizabeth went into the parlor and embraced Flora. "Mama, are you all right?"

"Yes, dear. You have to remember that your father is at peace and has finally completed his journey. We will all miss him so very much, but just imagine how happy he is now." Flora meant the words she spoke, but the tears continued to run down her thin face. "I'm afraid that Anna will not be strong enough to accept this. Elizabeth, you will have to help me with her."

"I will, Mama."

Only hours later, Anna, A. G., and the girls arrived. After greeting their grandma quietly, Simmy took the little ones back to the kitchen, where she had milk and tea cakes for them. Anna clung to Flora and wept for some time. Flora let her cry without interrupting. When the tears subsided, Flora patted her youngest daughter and whispered into her ear. "Do you think that Papa's life glorified God, Anna?"

"Yes, Mama, I do."

"Then he did his job here on this earth, and now he is receiving his reward."

To Anna, her mother's comment sounded just like one of Papa's catechism questions, and somehow, that gave her a little feeling of comfort. She could see her own girls' faces instead of her own and Elizabeth's listening to Papa's questions as they fidgeted.

Anna and A. G. had made plans to move back to Tehvah in order to help with the work on the place and care for Anna's aging parents. They would have to move forward with those plans now. Anna went into the kitchen, where the girls were having their tea cakes and milk. Anna looked at her girls as though she was seeing them for the very first time. She could plainly see her own face in Elizabeth, but Flora's curly, red hair clearly bore the mark of A. G.

Anna turned back toward the hall, remembering the last trip that she and Elizabeth had made together to Tehvah for the wedding. That time was memorable, because Papa was feeling well, and it was a happy occasion. She climbed the stairs and saw that Elizabeth was seated on their old bed. Anna sat down beside her sister and took her hand.

"We will always have wonderful memories, Anna." Anna was very quiet as she listened to the sound of Elizabeth's voice. She stared out the window, as she had no words to express her feeling of loss. She wondered how they could live a normal life at Tehvah without Papa. She would try hard not to think about Tehvah without her papa.

Anna looked up from her trance-like state. "Elizabeth, it seems like all the good things are being taken from this world, and we just continue to live in a place that never changes. People don't seem to care about anything or anybody but themselves. Papa at least tried to make this a better place for us to live."

"The real difference was Papa's love for the Lord, Anna." Anna looked up at Elizabeth, wiping her eyes.

"I know he sure tried to keep us headed in the right direction."

"I think that if everyone tried to obey God's laws as much as Papa did, this old world would be a much better place—not perfect, but better." Anna smiled a little, and her sister knew that she felt better.

Elizabeth and Anna went downstairs and followed Simmy and the girls into the backyard. Izzy was waiting to greet them. Being the oldest of three, Izzy told Anna that she would be glad to watch the girls for her.

"Oh, Lordy," said Simmy. "Just like ol' times again."

"I was just thinking the same thing," Elizabeth said, remembering how Simmy followed the two of them around the yard like an old mother hen.

Anna watched the girls run through the yard and toward the old hanging tree. "Simmy, does Izzy know the story about that tree where the man was hanged?" Elizabeth continued to watch as she saw Izzy pointing up at a high limb jutting out over the lawn.

"Sure she do. Ain't no tale we told she don't know."

Anna smiled to hear that her own girls were being filled in on all the old stories that she, Elizabeth, and Simmy had shared. "Looks like we have come full circle," Anna said.

"Yep, it's the end of an era, all right." Elizabeth walked back to the kitchen. The three old friends sat down at the kitchen table.

Anna seemed worried. "I'm not sure the girls understand about Papa's death. I just told them that he had gone home to be with Jesus."

"That just what he done." Simmy nodded her head in approval.

Elizabeth took up the conversation. "I think that was an excellent explanation, Anna. It was simple, and most of all, it was true."

People from the church began to bring food for the family and pay their respects to Flora and the girls. Cousins and extended family began to arrive and talk about old times and the days when they were all younger. By the time they had exchanged stories, the day was changed from one of gloom to a celebration of George Torrey's life. The family left in buggies for the church in town where Reverend Grafton would preach Papa's funeral and all the congregation would sing his favorite hymns.

The family sat in the pew in front of the coffin, recalling all the times they heard the gospel preached from that pulpit. The coffin rested where Elizabeth and Anna stood so many years ago and recited the catechism that Papa had helped them with when they were young. Anna recalled the preacher's dreaded five-point sermons and the Sunday that Mr. McEachern prayed so long for rain. Anna vowed then and there to teach her girls that catechism and make sure they were in that church each Sunday, as she and Elizabeth were. *Papa would have wanted that,* she thought.

The service was over, and the congregation stood for the benediction. Once outside, everyone climbed into their buggies and followed the carriage with Papa's body back to Tehvah for burial in the family cemetery alongside little Hugh, Grandpa and Grandma Torrey, and George's twin brothers. There were so many buggies that it seemed everyone in the town wanted to show respect for George.

As the hearse arrived, the soft, melodious strains of an old spiritual filled the air. The field hands and all George's black friends came to bid him farewell. "Deep river," they sang.

Anna wiped the tears from her eyes, "Oh, Papa would have loved this. Is that Zeb leading the singing?" As the mourners paid their last respects to George Torrey and began to leave, Elizabeth and Anna remained just outside the wrought iron fence where Papa was buried. They stared blankly at the new grave in the plot. The dirt was very dry from the lack of rain, and for some reason, this dry earth gave Anna an even greater sense of loss.

As they turned to walk back to the house, there was thunder in the distance. Even though the sun was shining to the west, small drops of rain began to fall on the thirsty ground. As each drop hit the dry ground, little puffs of dust floated silently into the air like so many spirits rising heavenward.

Elizabeth broke the silence. "Anna, do you remember when we asked Papa about the meaning of Tehvah?"

"Yes, and I remember how safe and loved we felt in that big old ark."

Anna's eyes, red and swollen from her grief, surveyed the eastern sky through the softly falling rain. "Look, Elizabeth."

"What is it, Anna?"

A feeling of peace swept through Anna as she pointed out the bright object in the distant sky. "It's a rainbow, Elizabeth. It's a rainbow." Anna smiled.

Until the final promise appears, we continue to live in a world of our own making on the other side of the flood.

CPSIA information can be obtained at www.ICGtesting.com
Printed in the USA
LVOW081054070213

318970LV00003B/5/P

9 781449 780715